"What's bothering you, Jenna?" Keith asked abruptly.

She shook her head. "You have an uncomfortable habit of reading my mind, and I wish you would stop." She pushed the hair from her forehead. "I made a fool of myself last night."

His lips twisted in a slight smile. "I was afraid you'd see it that way."

She studied his face. "Which is why you didn't come in with me?"

Giving a rough laugh, he said, "The way I feel now, it seems an incredibly stupid thing for me to have done."

She glanced away. "I don't make a habit of propositioning men, you know." Her voice was gruff with embarrassment. "In fact, it was my first time."

"Don't you think I know that?" He sounded annoyed she'd felt it necessary to explain. "Don't you know that I've seen what's at the heart of you, Jenna?"

Then he added, "Nothing happened last night that should cause you shame. So you can stop building those walls. Be warned, Jenna. I'll knock them down, every last one of them."

Then he smiled and put a hand on her cheek. "Stop looking for complications."

Shaking her head, she said, "Wait a minute. Lord, it seems like I'm always saying that to you. But I don't know what's going on. I don't know—"

The rest of her protest was lost against his lips as he pressed her back to the grass. There was no wall between them now. Nothing except an explosion of emotion that made ̶ ̶ ̶ ̶ ̶ ̶ ̶ ̶ ̶ ̶ ̶ ̶ ̶ tion, every doubt. This ̶ ̶ ̶ ̶ ̶ vow. . . .

WHAT ARE *LOVESWEPT* ROMANCES?

They are stories of true romance and touching emotion. We believe those two very important ingredients are constants in our highly sensual and very believable stories in the *LOVESWEPT* line. Our goal is to give you, the reader, stories of consistently high quality that may sometimes make you laugh, sometimes make you cry, but are always fresh and creative and contain many delightful surprises within their pages.

Most romance fans read an enormous number of books. Those they truly love, they keep. Others may be traded with friends and soon forgotten. We hope that each *LOVESWEPT* romance will be a treasure—a "keeper." We will always try to publish

LOVE STORIES YOU'LL NEVER FORGET
BY AUTHORS YOU'LL ALWAYS REMEMBER

The Editors

Loveswept ® 564

Billie Green
Man from the Mist

BANTAM BOOKS
NEW YORK · TORONTO · LONDON · SYDNEY · AUCKLAND

MAN FROM THE MIST

A Bantam Book / September 1992

If you would be interested in receiving protective vinyl
covers for your Loveswept books, please write to this address
for information:

Loveswept
Bantam Books
P.O. Box 985
Hicksville, NY 11802

ISBN 0-553-44246-5

Published simultaneously in the United States and Canada

Bantam Books are published by Bantam Books, a division of
Bantam Doubleday Dell Publishing Group, Inc. Its trademark,
consisting of the words "Bantam Books" and the portrayal of
a rooster, is Registered in U.S. Patent and Trademark Office
and in other countries. Marca Registrada. Bantam Books, 666
Fifth Avenue, New York, New York 10103.

PRINTED IN THE UNITED STATES OF AMERICA

OPM   0 9 8 7 6 5 4 3 2 1

Author Note

A long time ago while I was reading a Georgette Heyer Regency novel, I came across three very beautiful words: asthore, acushla, and alanna. I didn't know what they meant—I still don't, in fact—but since the hero of the book, who happened to be Irish, murmured them to his beloved, I guessed that they were Irish terms of endearment. The words have stayed with me through all these years, and now, with MAN FROM THE MIST, I finally have *my* own Irish hero saying these very same words to his beloved.

One

It was all Myron's fault.

Shifting her position on the rocky ledge, Jenna exhaled a small, irate puff of air. This whole thing was Myron Appleton's fault.

Several wisps of Jenna's black hair had escaped the French braid to curl around her face; her almond-shaped eyes had gone from violet to the color of the sky at midnight; her black jeans were covered with dust; and there was a corner tear in the shoulder of her brand-new, lavender wool blouse. And it was all Myron's fault.

Dipping her head slightly, she stared with narrowed eyes at the rip in her blouse. Gradually, as she thought of the man who was responsible, the heat of righteous indignation sent strength through her small frame and color to her cheeks.

"Listen to me, sweetness. If you can have those designs ready for me in two weeks, I'll be able to take them to Chicago. I'll get massive orders . . . and money. You'll get national recognition . . . and

money. Before you know it, we'll both be too rich and famous to speak to each other."

"Not having to speak to you ever again would be heaven on earth, Myron, but you know damn well—"

"Yes, yes, it's late notice, and I wouldn't ask this of anyone else. But I know you, Jenna. You do your best work under pressure."

Myron, with his so-exclusive interior-decorating salon and his so-devious mind, was responsible for the mess she found herself in now, Jenna told herself as she pressed closer to the rock face.

Myron always knew exactly what he wanted and exactly how to get it. He had sweet-talked Jenna into working night and day to complete his order for a set of new spring designs. Facets of her design would be picked out and incorporated into linen for bed and bath, into upholstery and drapery fabric, and wallpaper and borders.

And because Jenna had never learned how to give anything less than her best, she not only had worked around the clock on the drawings, but had made frenzied trips to the textile factory that would turn her drawings into reality, flattering a foul-tempered manager, forcing herself to be diplomatic to people who seemed determined to ruin her.

It was as Jenna had drawn near the end of the rush assignment that the dizzy spells had begun. Spinning rooms were disconcerting, but she could have lived with them. She could have adjusted if she hadn't had the Other Symptom to contend with.

The Other Symptom had frightened her. Worse, it had embarrassed her. She couldn't bring herself to think about it in broad daylight. And she had refused to discuss it even with the receptionist who had booked her appointment with Dr. Weston, the general practitioner who had been in charge of Jenna's health for most of her twenty-six years.

"Dr. Weston." Jenna almost lost her grip on the rock as she straightened her back abruptly.

Myron may have been a catalyst, but Dr. Frank Weston was the real offender. Why hadn't she thought of it before? The whole thing was Dr. Weston's fault.

"You're worn out, Jenna. You've been working nonstop for eighteen months. No one can do what you've been doing without paying for it sooner or later. Tranquilizers will help, but they're only a temporary measure at best. You have to have peace and quiet. No stress. No pressure. Absolutely no work for at least a month. We can only hope you've done yourself no permanent damage."

It was Dr. Weston, with his deceptively humble voice and his pseudofatherly concern, who had shoved Jenna into her present predicament. If the good doctor hadn't scared her with his talk of stress-related illnesses and the consequences of pushing her mind and body too hard, if he hadn't insisted she take a complete break from her work, Jenna would still be in Dallas, with its comfortably familiar glass and concrete towers. If Dr. Weston hadn't used scare tactics, Jenna would never have listened to Dink and—

"Dink!" Jenna squeaked, changing her mind yet again as the situation finally became clear.

The source of her trouble wasn't Myron. Nor was it dear old Dr. Weston. It was Georgiana Harte Aldham, alias Dink the Fink.

"You've got to come, Jenna. What's the use of having one's husband inherit an Irish castle if one can't lord it over one's friends? How in hell am I supposed to play lady of the manor without an appreciative audience? For heaven's sake, Jenna, noblesse oblige doesn't work if there are no commoners around to oblige."

"Dink, I can't. I'm too busy. How can one support oneself if one doesn't work? Couldn't I just bow and scrape and pull my forelock over the phone?"

"Are you doing something different with your hair? You've got to come. A castle, Jenna. A castle of my very own. You know how I've always wanted one. And now that poor depraved Uncle Edward has gone to his reward, I'm Lady Aldham. Who woulda thunk it? You do see why you've got to come. It's no good my doing my duchess imitation if I don't have anyone to giggle with later."

Jenna had held out against Dink's wheedling for several months. She had held out until the fourth time she had sat huddling against her drawing board in the middle of the night, shivering and shaking, her body drenched in cold sweat as she fought the Other Symptom.

So Jenna had gone to London, but within minutes of her arrival she realized the calm atmosphere prescribed by the good doctor couldn't have been farther away. Thanks to Dink, Jenna was immediately thrown into a whirlwind of parties, sightseeing, and shopping. Calm didn't live in the same house with Sir Geoffrey's lady.

In a sane, rational world, the marital entity that was Dink and Geoffrey could not have existed. Geoffrey, a nicely rounded, comfortable man, was all discretion and suitability. Dink, curvaceous, blond, and hyperactive, was all impulsive will-o'-the-wisp, a Texas version of a Valley Girl.

Together the unlikely couple had produced two amazingly normal children, Jeff and Amelia. Geoffrey's main contribution to the children's up-bringing was Mrs. Hargreaves, the stern-faced nanny who had raised him. Dink's contributions included a Jenna Howard nursery, Woody Allen movies, and regular demonstrations of the routine that had won her a place as head cheerleader in the ninth grade.

In Dink's company Jenna's three days in London had not been restful, they had not been quiet, and they had not been stress-free. Therefore by the time the small, noisy group—minus Geoffrey, who would join them later—boarded the plane for Ireland, Jenna had been praying for boredom.

She didn't find it. No reasonable human being could find Ireland boring. It was even more beautiful than Jenna had imagined.

After landing at Shannon Airport they were driven in an ancient Rolls-Royce by an equally ancient chauffeur through the countryside, passing rolling green hills and pristine loughs, white-washed cottages and movie-set villages.

It was a dream come to life. A dream that was disrupted just a little by Jenna's first glimpse of Aldham Castle.

Following Dink's instructions, the driver had stopped the Rolls on a rise about a quarter of a mile from the castle so that Jenna would have a chance to admire the aged edifice in the fading light. The children, from either cowardice or fatigue, chose to stay in the car with Mrs. Hargreaves.

"Dear sweet heaven." Jenna's eyes were wide and wary as she stood beside the car and leaned her head back to see all the way to the top of the towering, sprawling, glowering, hulking stone structure.

"That is the ugliest thing I've ever seen in my life," she said bluntly.

"Yes, isn't it?" Unreasonable Dink seemed pleased by the insult. "It's drafty and damp and smells like something that's been left too long at the bottom of the laundry hamper. A real castle."

Managing with difficulty to pull her gaze away from the looming black battlements, Jenna glanced at the blond woman standing beside her. "Dink, really, it can't be safe," she said warily. "I mean, have you checked for root rot and that kind of thing?"

Dink gave a gurgling laugh. "It's perfectly safe. Scout's honor. Castles aren't exactly disposable things. Those old Celts knew what they were doing. They built these suckers to last."

"Pity," Jenna muttered.

The interior of Aldham Castle wasn't much better than the exterior. On the other side of the massive, nail-studded front door were marble floors, tapestry-lined walls, and chandeliers that would have sent any cleaning woman of Jenna's acquaintance screaming into the night.

Months before, Dink had begun the process of renovation. Downstairs, two dining rooms and three drawing rooms, the billiard room and the solarium, Geoffrey's study and the kitchen, had been made fit for human habitation. On the second floor eight of the bedrooms as well as the nursery suite had been brought, kicking and screaming by the looks of them, into the twentieth century.

On that first evening, events had progressed as normally as possible under the circumstances—circumstances that included a bathtub deep enough to give you the bends if you came up too quickly, a water pump that knocked with an uncomfortably urgent rhythm, and truly ugly purple bath towels that flaunted the ornate Aldham crest. But on Jenna's second day in Ireland things began to go awry.

After lunch Dink—pregnant *again*—went to her room for her usual nap, and Mrs. Hargreaves, with all the warmth and humor of a cartoon mortician, refused to let Jenna disrupt the children's routine with her unsavory American presence.

Which was why Jenna had been left to her own devices, and why she decided to explore the unused rooms of the castle. And it was why, as she peered into nooks and crannies that surely hadn't seen the light of day in centuries, she heard something that sent her rushing out of the castle, away from the Other Symptom. . . .

"And it was all Dink's fault," Jenna said aloud, her voice strong with conviction.

If her addlepated friend hadn't insisted on marrying Geoffrey Aldham, none of it would have happened. There would be no children and no tyrannical nanny; there wouldn't have been another pregnancy requiring naps; there would have been no castle with shadows and whistling currents of air, no creepy places for the Other Symptom to hide.

Without Dink's interference Jenna would have

gone to Bora Bora for a holiday, like any normal person. And she wouldn't now be six feet off the ground on a rocky ledge, trapped by a pack of bloodthirsty animals.

"They're sheep," Jenna reminded herself in disgust. "Overgrown lambs, for heaven's sake. What are they going to do, nibble me to death?"

But of course logic had nothing to do with fear. Jenna knew only two things about sheep: They smelled bad, and she didn't trust them. Not for a minute.

This shouldn't be happening, she told herself. Not to Jenna Howard, astute businesswoman and innovative designer. Not to a woman whose after-dinner imitations of Liza Minnelli and Charlie Chaplin were almost famous; a woman who could speak knowledgeably on politics, sports, science, and the arts; a woman who could, with a couple of wine coolers under her belt, bend her thumbs back to touch her wrists.

"Multitalented people are not supposed to go around hugging rocks for the entertainment of farm animals," she muttered.

A moment later when she caught movement out of the corner of her eyes, Jenna tore her gaze away from the milling sheep. A man was walking across the pasture, on a course perpendicular to the ledge.

Although he was too far away for her to see his features, Jenna became instantly aware of the self-confidence in his long stride, self-confidence that was somehow comforting even from a distance.

Gripping the rock face with one hand, she waved the other one above her head. "Hello there!"

she called out. "Hello. Do you think you could help me out?"

The man stopped abruptly and, turning his head, gazed across the field at her for a moment. Then he began to move her way. When he reached the milling sheep, he simply pushed his way through, speaking softly but firmly to the animals until he stood directly below her.

Jenna's first impression was that he was a brown man—brown hair, brown eyes, brown jacket, and deeply tanned skin. His high forehead, Roman nose, and eyes that drooped at the outer corners gave him a look of gentle authority. He wasn't male-model pretty or male-model crisp, but there was something compelling about the lean face that was still turned up to her.

He didn't speak. He merely stood there, quietly staring. He stared so long and so steadily that Jenna's relief began to turn to discomfort.

Then, as she gazed down at him in growing confusion, his strong lips twisted in a strange, off-center smile. "So you've finally come, then," he said slowly.

Two

"Are the sheep blocking your way back into the hill?" the stranger asked, his voice casual as he continued to study Jenna's face.

"No," she said slowly. "No, they're blocking my way off this ledge and out of this bucolic nightmare."

He chuckled. "Perhaps I can help."

Grasping her waist with both hands, he lifted her off the ledge as though she weighed nothing at all, and with economical movements brought one arm under her knees and began to walk back through the milling sheep.

"I feel so silly," she murmured. "I don't know why they took it into their heads to follow me, like something out of Fractured Fairy Tales or maybe Little Bopeep, Mel Brooks–style."

"It's their nature to follow," he explained. "They're slow-witted beasts, but harmless enough."

"Easy for you to say. You obviously live with

the creatures. We don't have them in Dallas . . . at least not in my part of town."

A glint of amusement shone in his dark eyes. "I can't precisely say I *live* with them. They're only allowed into the house on special occasions, you see."

Against her will she laughed. It was against her will because she definitely did *not* want to be amused by this eccentric stranger, any more than she wanted to be fascinated by the soft, lyrical sound of his voice and the warmth in his brown eyes.

Jenna had met quite a few men in her twenty-six years—men of wealth and power, men who were loaded with charm and good looks—but other than her ex-fiancé, she had felt nothing more than a fleeting interest in any one of them. Why now, when she was smack in the middle of this rustic refuge, with a man who tended sheep and, given her luck, was more than likely unbalanced, should she be feeling a definite little zing of attraction?

Spinning rooms . . . the Other Symptom . . . screwball nobility . . . crumbling Irish castles . . . fascinating, off-the-wall shepherds.

Is it my imagination, she wondered silently, *or is my life suddenly taking on a bizarre new texture?*

A moment later, when Jenna glanced around, she found that they were well clear of the sheep. But she was still in his arms, and he was still walking.

She cleared her throat. "Excuse me . . . excuse me. It was really sweet of you to help me. I don't know what I would have done if you hadn't come along. Turned into a local legend, I guess:

the crazy tourist who stands on a ledge muttering, 'No more sheep . . . no more sheep.' But, well, the thing is, you can put me down now."

Murmuring "If you like," he sat her on her feet, brushed a strand of dark hair from her cheek, and then he was staring again, with what looked like a combination of surprise and pleasure, amusement and warm welcome.

She opened her mouth to say something, to voice an objection even though she still wasn't quite sure what she was objecting to, but she stopped short when he took her arm in his and began to walk with her slowly across the meadow in the same direction from which he had come.

Jenna glanced at him from the corner of her eyes, then caught her lower lip between her teeth. Now what? She came from a world filled with meaningless talk. Every upwardly mobile young professional came supplied with a stock set of words and phrases that could be adapted to suit every occasion, business or personal. It was somewhat lowering to realize that out of her environment, Jenna had to think harder. And before she could find the right words, words that would convey both gratitude and dismissal, he beat her to the punch and broke the silence.

"So what is it you call yourself?"

Irish chitchat? "That depends on my mood," she said dryly. "Sometimes I call myself genius and sometimes I call myself stupid bitch." When he laughed, she added, "I was born Jenna Annelle Grafton Howard, but Jenna will do."

"Jenna." His head was cocked slightly to one side as though he were listening to the sound of her name. "Jenna," he said again. "There's a gentle feel to it, like sunshine in early spring, all warm and soft to ease the chill of winter away." He smiled at her. "Hello, Jenna, I'm Keith Donegal."

His steps slowed, then stopped as he looked down at her, a frown bringing deep creases to his tanned face. "Do you like it? My name, I mean."

"It's a . . . a nice name."

"That's good, then. It's the only name I've got. It would be a worry if you didn't like it."

"Sure it would," she agreed slowly, then glanced around. She didn't recognize anything around her, and she was almost sure this wasn't the way she had come. "Keith, where—"

"Say it again," he interrupted.

Jenna glanced down at the strong fingers on her arm, then at his face. She moistened her lips in a nervous gesture. "I beg your pardon?"

"Will you say my name again?"

Bloodthirsty sheep were looking better and better. Swallowing heavily, she said, "Keith?"

He shook his head, murmuring, "To think I've heard the name all these years, never knowing it could sound like that."

She let out a slow breath. "I'm glad you like the way I say your name, but—"

"You make it sound an ordinary thing. It isn't. Not at all. It's a little piece of magic you've given me, with me not expecting it at all." He laughed softly, then, taking her hand, he began to walk again. "I should have known."

Across the field Jenna spied a farmhouse and suddenly dug in her heels. Humoring an eccentric was one thing. Following him into confined quarters was something else entirely.

"Hold on a second," she said firmly. "Listen to

me. I don't know what's going on—you lost me about two seconds after you walked through the sheep—but I refuse to move another inch until you answer some questions. And don't you dare go off into Never-Never Land again. I want straight answers, and I want them *now.*"

When his lips curved in that slow smile of his, Jenna steeled herself against him and focused on annoyance. The idiot was looking at her as though she were *cute,* she thought in disgust. He obviously didn't know about Jenna's reputation as a shrew extraordinaire. She might be only five foot two, but judicious people quailed when they received the look Jenna was giving Keith now.

"Such as?" he asked.

It took a moment for her to realize that he was referring to her demands. "Such as—well, such as what did you mean when you said I've 'finally come, then'?" she asked, imitating his Irish brogue.

"Have y'been to Ireland before?"

Why did the question sound like an accusation? "No," she said hesitantly. "I've always wanted to. I've read a lot about it, but I've never been here."

"Then don't you think it's well and gone past time? Our Erin's a special land, Jenna. Not a place for reading about. It's a place for feeling yourself." His thumb moved on the underside of her arm in a delicate stroke. "Don't you feel it right now?"

She stared up at him. *Oh, I feel it all right,* she admitted silently. But it wasn't Ireland that caused the frisson of pleasure that raced through her system. It was a single, innocent touch.

She cleared her throat. "I suppose my run-in with the sheep was a pretty good clue that I'm a newcomer," she conceded reluctantly, "but you said something else . . . something about the sheep blocking my way into the hill."

"Fairies live under that hill," he explained, his voice matter-of-fact. "When I saw you there, with your hair black as soot and your skin like fresh, sweet cream, and you no bigger than could sit in the palm of my hand, I was that sure you were one of them, tryin' to get back in. Maybe even the queen of the fairies herself."

"Of course you did," she said, stealing a sideways glance at him. "Why don't you just tell me where you're taking me? Whose house is that, and why are we here?"

"It's my house. Donegal Farm. And we're here because it's time for tea." Urging her forward, he began to stride forward again.

It wasn't her fault, Jenna assured herself as she walked beside him. He had been across a field when she had hailed him. How could she have known then that he was simpleminded? Sweet and charming but very definitely simpleminded.

And it was the sweetness that had her meekly following where he led. As though she weren't a hard-nosed, hardheaded, nineties kind of woman. As though she didn't have a cast-iron will of her own. She was doing it out of sheer generosity of spirit. After all Jenna Howard could be as altruistic as the next guy.

They entered the farmhouse through the back door, walking directly into the kitchen. For a moment she thought some decorator had gone overboard with "authentic" rustic charm, then she realized that this wasn't artificial authenticity. This was the real McCoy. The huge, black stove, the slate sink, the wooden counters—these things hadn't been picked up at an auction. These things had always been a part of Donegal Farm.

While Jenna sat at a heavy wooden table, Keith worked at the counter with economical movements, making tea, slicing bread, and spreading each thick slice with butter. As he worked, he spoke quietly, his soft brogue putting her at ease, subtly seducing her into feeling comfortable. He spoke of uncomplicated things, of innocent things. The weather and the sheep, how the crops and his neighbors were faring.

As Jenna listened, her eyes slowly narrowed. "Wait a minute," she interrupted, her voice indignant. "You're not simpleminded."

"Is it a requirement?" He raised one heavy brow in inquiry. "Was it a dolt you were looking for?"

"No . . . no, that's all right." She pushed back a curl in a nervous gesture. "You can be intelligent if you want."

"That's good, then." He placed a tray of bread and butter on the table beside the teapot. "You spoke of Dallas earlier. Would that be Dallas, Texas, over in America?"

"Is there another one?"

"And you make your home there? It's a wonder, that. Dallas, Texas." He spoke the words softly, with awe, but there was a suspicious sparkle in his dark eyes. "Cattle and cowboys. Sure and wouldn't I like to see such a sight."

Jenna studied the innocent look for a long, silent moment. She looked away, then back again. "I think I'm getting it," she said finally. "Slow but sure, that's me. Not only are you not slow-witted, you're not even Irish. Where're you from, Brooklyn?"

He grinned. "You're, like, way off base, dude."

"California?" Although she tried to be angry, she couldn't quite pull it off. His American smile was as powerful as his Irish one had been. "Leave it to me to run into a fake Irishman."

When he threw back his head and laughed, the deep, rich sound reached all the way inside her, stroking the hidden parts.

"Not fake," he finally said in denial. "I was born here, right here in County Limerick, but when I was twelve, I moved with my mother to L.A." He pulled out a chair, turned it around, and straddled it, leaning his forearms on the back. "Eat your bread and butter. Mrs. Kennedy is off to see her sick cousin, or I could offer you better."

"This is fine," she murmured, then met his eyes. "How long have you been back?"

"Five years." Something about those five years seemed to bother him, but only for a moment. He smiled and said, "I didn't really intend to pull your leg with the Irish brogue. It seems I've become Irish again."

"You live here permanently now?"

"This is my home. I was born in this house and I'll probably die here." He shifted his position slightly. "Now let's talk about you. What do you do over in Dallas, Texas, USA?"

Leaning back in her chair, she found she was beginning to relax again. "I create charming little designs—don't laugh, now—for household linen and wallpaper."

"Why should I laugh? Everyone has a secret wish to be an artist of some kind, but not everyone is given the gift. You should be proud."

"An artist?" She gave a doubtful laugh. "It's nice

of you to say so, but if you have to put a label on it, I guess you would call me an artisan, a skilled craftsman."

"These designs, are they good?"

Jenna considered the question carefully. "Yes . . . yes, they are. My stuff has really caught on in the last couple of years. I'm suddenly in demand. Which is why—"

She broke off and became totally involved in taking a bite of bread and butter.

"Why what?"

She shrugged and took a sip of the strong, hot tea. "You've got to take advantage of popularity," she explained. "Things change too fast. If people want a Jenna Howard design, I have to give it to them before they decide someone else is the *in* designer. So I pushed myself too hard. I cashed in on the demand until I hit burnout. Stress city. It happens to most people sooner or later."

"Then why does it bother you so much?"

Jenna glanced away from him. She had purposely kept her voice casual. He wasn't supposed to see that she was uneasy. A stranger wasn't supposed to know that much about her.

"Why are you asking so many questions?" she muttered.

"Jenna." The word was a gentle scold.

After a small hesitation she exhaled slowly. "Okay, okay. It worries me because I had a small—itsy-bitsy, really—breakdown. All my energy packed up and left." She gave a short laugh. "Like a rat deserting a sinking ship. I woke up every morning feeling like Dracula had visited me in the middle of the night. And I couldn't work. I had plenty of wonderful ideas, but somehow my poor brain had forgotten how to send signals to my fingers."

When she realized her hands were shaking, she dropped them to her lap and smiled. "But it wasn't any big deal. Not really. It happens to people all the time. Dr. Weston said all I needed was a little peace and quiet. No work. No stress."

He was silent for a moment. "Something's scaring you," he said finally. "Not the fatigue or the inability to work. It's something else."

Sighing, she pushed a lock of hair from her forehead. "No, you're right. That stuff was bad, but just ordinary. The Other Symptom shook me up a little, but—"

Breaking off, she stared at him, her eyes wide. "Why am I telling you this? I haven't even told Dink. There's nothing worse than forcing a perfect stranger to listen to your medical problems. Mrs. Cross, a woman who lives in my apartment building, every time she gets into the elevator where she *knows* no one can escape her, insists on giving every detail of her gallbladder surgery. I always pray she won't get to the drainage problems before we reach the lobby. I can't believe I was about to do exactly the same thing to—"

"The Other Symptom?" he urged patiently.

She glanced out the window, exhaled slowly, then muttered something under her breath.

"Speak up, asthore, I can't hear you when you mumble like that."

She turned back to him. His smile was amused and determined, but, incredibly, there was also understanding there.

Straightening her shoulders, she said, "I said I saw things that other people couldn't see and I heard things that other people couldn't hear." The words came out in a rush, and she was tempted to add, *So there.*

As silence fell between them, Jenna watched his face. He didn't look shocked, as her business manager had when she told him; he didn't look wary, like the few of her friends who knew; and he didn't seem to be bracing himself in case she decided to freak out, the way her parents had after Dr. Weston talked to them. Keith simply looked interested.

"Tell me about it," he said quietly.

Frowning, she wondered what his angle was. There had to be an angle. No one was this nice.

With her arms folded on the table, she leaned closer. "One night, when I was working on my last assignment—it was about three in the morning and I hadn't had more than eight hours of sleep in the preceding three days. I was running on caffeine and willpower. Anyway I looked up and . . . well, the figures on the wallpaper in my studio—figures *I* designed—began to kind of . . . move around."

Her voice had faded away to a whisper. Glancing up, she met his eyes and realized she still hadn't shocked him, so she brushed the hair from her forehead again, looked him in the eyes, and brought out the big guns.

"The blasted designs moved, and they changed. I swear to God they changed. They were beautiful, exotic, and whimsical, like something from an-other world. But they were not *my* creations. I was pretty groggy, you understand, so at first I was excited and wanted to get what I was seeing down on paper before it all disappeared. But eventually I realized what was happening."

Jenna smiled grimly. "I had, quietly, and in the comfort and privacy of my own home, gone right around the bend."

"Is that right?" he said, his voice polite.

Jenna's fingers clenched when she saw he was hiding a smile. He knew she was trying to shake him, and he was determined not to be shaken.

"You're being so understanding just to irritate me, aren't you?" she accused in exasperation. "As a matter of fact that's not all. I heard voices." *How do you like them apples?* she thought with smug belligerence. "It sounded like the Three Little Pigs were having a party in my head. They were laughing and talking. A whole gaggle . . . or pack or herd, I don't know the term for an assemblage of hallucinations. One time I even heard the little monsters singing. I couldn't hear distinct words, but they seemed to be having a real good time."

"How many times did that happen?"

"Four nights spread out through a week. They hung on until I decided to visit Dink, then they left. But they took all my strength with them," she said wryly. "The cunning little things stole my energy and my peace of mind and left me feeling like a freak."

He shook his head, a sorrowful movement. "You've let it grow out of proportion." When she opened her mouth to object, he stopped her with a look. "You're in Ireland now, Jenna. You tell anyone you meet what you've just told me and they'll simply nod and pull up a story that'll leave yours in the dust."

"Are you trying to tell me that everyone in Ireland is schizoid?"

"Let's call it peculiar," he said, grinning. "And that's just the world citizen in me talking. The Irish in me would tell you that you've had a run-in with the Little People."

She coughed, choking on air and surprise. "The . . . the Little People?"

"Leprechauns," he said in an offhand way. "Don't give me that look. We've already established the fact that I'm sane. The voices and the designs changing—those things worried you because you didn't understand, but a true Irishman would feel shame if he hadn't heard from the Folk Under the Hill at least once in his life."

What a sweet man, she thought, intrigued against her will. *A sweet, thoroughly strange man.* He was trying to make her feel better. The surprising part was, she did. When she realized the tightness in her neck and shoulders was gone, she gave a soft laugh of relief.

"So the Wee Folk visited you, all the way over in Dallas, Texas?" He smiled in pleasure. "And because of it you decided to visit Ireland to find what you've been looking for. Is that right?"

"I guess you could put it that way," she said doubtfully. "It certainly sounds better than saying I popped my clutch."

He laughed. "And how do you like staying up at the castle with Lady Georgiana?"

She wasn't surprised that he knew. Ireland or Texas, a small town was a small town.

"I'm not sure," she said after a moment. "The halls moan, the windows whistle, and the shadows move." She bit her lip. "In fact the reason I found myself being terrorized by those stupid sheep was because I was running away from the castle. Just before I left, I swear I heard something rustling in the shadows, something that moved quickly, something not quite real. I thought I left that kind of thing back in Dallas."

"Rats?" he suggested.

"Not unless Irish rats giggle," she said dryly. "And if they do, I may start sleeping with Jeff and Amelia." She shook her head. "I don't like it. The noises, the moving shadows, unknown things lurking in the corridors."

He laughed. "All castles are like that. And if the small rustlings sent you out to me, they couldn't be anything but kind spirits."

"They didn't sound kind. They sounded damned hair-raising." She glanced around his kitchen. "I like this better. There's a warm, welcoming feeling to it."

As their eyes met, she could see—she could almost *feel*—the burst of pleasure that shook through him, showing in his lean face. Then an instant later the atmosphere wasn't simply warm, it was downright hot. As she stared into his dark eyes, she felt . . . She didn't know quite what she felt, but it was certainly something she had never felt before.

Then without warning, without reason, Jenna's chest constricted painfully and she felt tears form, burning her eyes. Something about this man brought childhood memories rushing up to meet her, memories of wanting to be held in someone's arms, but not just an ordinary embrace. She had wanted to be held tightly. She had wanted to be held emphatically. She had wanted to be held in an embrace that meant something.

During her teen years her needs had become more focused. At night when she lay awake in bed, she would wrap her arms around her body and hug herself. Because there was no one else to do it. She would feel herself mentally reaching out for something, reaching out to *someone* out there in the big, unknown world. Someone who could soothe away her aching need for love and acceptance.

As Jenna stared at Keith in stunned silence, she saw an awareness in his eyes, as though he had shared her memories, shared her pain. And when he moved, the idea took hold that he was going to fold her into his arms to comfort her. She almost swayed toward him. Almost.

Instead she blinked twice, and instantly everything was back to normal. He was once again a nice man who had shared his tea with a stranger. Nothing more.

"I guess I'd better get back," she said, thankful that her voice sounded so normal.

Keith pushed back his chair and rose to his feet. "I'll walk with you." He smiled. "You may need me to keep the vicious, wild creatures at bay."

She laughed, and her laughter surprised her. Jenna didn't usually let anyone tease her. Being female and small, she had developed pugilistic tendencies as early as kindergarten. She knew her personality had to be big and emphatic to make up for her size and, later on in business, to make up for her sex. But with Keith her automatic pilot didn't seem to work. There was no way she could resent the gentle teasing.

During their time in the kitchen a light rain had begun to fall, and a mist had formed, but Jenna didn't mind. It was a part of Ireland, as was the man who walked beside her. As they made idle conversation, Jenna watched him watching her and wondered what he thought of her, the inept tourist who had landed among his sheep.

Keith cut his eyes toward the woman walking beside him, wondering if she could have any idea of the throng of emotions that were doing battle inside him. Did she know that her appearance had knocked the breath out of him?

It was so strange that she should turn up now, he thought. It was almost funny. Almost.

As soon as he left her at the castle, he would visit his father's grave. He would tell him about the hair, as black and lustrous as a raven's wing. He would tell him about the violet eyes and the complexion, as smooth and pale as cream. The old man would have to see the humor of it. He would appreciate the irony. Maybe.

But as Keith drew in a long, slow breath, he changed his mind. Sean Donegal wouldn't have considered her appearance to be one of life's little jokes. Keith could almost see that weather-beaten face now, the dark eyes as solemn as the grave.

How's that for a little macabre humor, Da? Solemn as the grave . . . get it?

With an effort Keith shook free of the somber mood. There was no need for him to go off the deep end over this. It hurt a little to think of lost time and lost opportunities, but that couldn't be helped. Since his father wasn't here to guide him, he would simply have to play the hand as it was dealt.

. . .

When Keith left her at the door, Jenna didn't go inside immediately. For some reason she wasn't quite ready for the episode to end, so she stepped back into the shadows of the recessed doorway and watched him as he walked away from the castle.

He was a strange man, strange and fascinating, she told herself as he moved into the swirling mist. The edges of his man-shape began to grow indistinct. And then his solidity—the physical essence of him—began to waver, as though he were becoming a part of the mist. Seconds later, as Jenna watched, he was gone.

"Brigadoon," Jenna whispered unsteadily.

It wouldn't have surprised her to learn that Keith Donegal wouldn't reappear for another hundred years. What surprised her, what had her leaning heavily against the door for support, was the fact that for one moment, for one brief instant, Jenna had wanted to run after him. She had wanted to yell, *Wait for me. Let me come with you.*

Three

When Jenna woke up the following morning, her world was back to normal, or as normal as it could get in an Irish castle. The mist was gone, from the land and from her head, and she found she didn't quite believe in Keith Donegal.

There may have been a man who had rescued her from the sheep and given her tea, but he was just an ordinary man. The rest—the irresistible warmth, the immediate kinship—had been nothing more than the products of an exhausted mind.

Since getting back to reality was a code Jenna lived by, she was more than a little relieved to find herself on solid ground again, solid ground that suddenly was accompanied by the sounds of activity from the courtyard below.

Driven by reluctant curiosity, Jenna climbed out of bed and walked to the window.

Below her two cars—the Rolls and a faded blue Daimler—were being emptied of passengers and luggage. She couldn't tell how many passengers the vehicles contained, but she could see the luggage. Piles of luggage. Either a well-dressed army had arrived at Aldham Castle or someone was planning to stay a long, long time.

Jenna vaguely recalled that Dink had mentioned the possibility of other houseguests—that had been in London while Jenna was still suffering from jet lag and party fatigue—and as she gazed down into the courtyard, she felt, in equal parts, interest and irritation.

Although she wanted the peace and quiet Dr. Weston had prescribed for her, she knew herself well enough to realize that having too much time on her hands was not a good thing. So, after working her hair into a French braid, Jenna pulled on white linen slacks and a pale green cotton sweater and cautiously made her way downstairs.

By the time she arrived at the small dining room, a breakfast buffet had been set up on the sideboard, and the room seemed to be overflowing with people. But after Dink's elegantly offhanded introductions, the crowd broke up into only five new individuals.

The Coombs, Cecil and Anne, were an older couple. They wore matching tweed jackets, matching brown shoes, and had hair the same color of faded wheat. In their faces was the same banked glow of contentment. Jenna liked them immediately. They were the kind of people who, without effort, added genteel warmth to any gathering.

The second couple was a different can of worms. Not even in her thoughts did Jenna call them the Glendening-Waites because they were in no way unified. They were Maxwell Glendening-Waite and Carolyn Glendening-Waite, and they seemed to be doing their best to take away the warmth generated by the Coombs.

Carolyn Glendening-Waite was a tall, slender redhead and had the cool, untouchable look that only upper-class British women manage to achieve. Several adjectives could have been used to describe Carolyn—*elegant, sophisticated, exquisite*—but the one that came instantly to mind was *expensive*.

Carolyn's husband, Maxwell Glendening-Waite, Jenna instantly labeled the Fitzgerald Man. He possessed the kind of sharply defined good looks and languid movements that reminded Jenna of the self-absorbed decadence of the twenties. Like his wife, Max was tall and slender, and on the surface he was as cool as she was. But Jenna caught a glimpse of something else, some intense, but suppressed emotion that occasionally flared in his ice-blue eyes.

Max and Carolyn seemed to be bright and witty, and both spoke with a razor-edged, intellectual charm. They should have been a perfect match, but the looks that passed between the couple could have turned molten lava into cold, solid rock.

The last member of the group was a single man. Ralph Chambers was not handsome—he might even have been described as homely—but Ralph had attributes that were worth more than good looks. He was friendly and amusing, and he was an American. Ralph, born and raised in Kansas City, Missouri, had met Geoffrey through their mutual interest in the stock market, and the two had quickly become friends.

Add one slightly cracked artist manqúe to the group, Jenna thought as she sat beside Dink at the breakfast table, and you came up with an interesting mixture of houseguests.

"No, of course not," Cecil said, laying his napkin across his plate. "Anne and I aren't tired at all. On the contrary, we find the country air wonderfully invigorating." Cecil glanced at the other couple. "What about you, Max?"

For the past ten minutes Max had been staring a hole in Jenna and, without taking his eyes from her, he said, "Always ready, Cecil, always ready. You'll find I'm game for any amusement"—he smiled as he said the word—" that Lady Georgiana has devised for us."

"Say what?" Jenna muttered under her breath, then rose to her feet and walked to the sideboard for more coffee.

"I found a croquet set in the game room." Dink, her eyes sparkling with hidden amusement, glanced around the table. "What do you think?"

"Croquet?" Carolyn arched one slender brow in elegant incredulity.

"Splendid" was Cecil's enthusiastic response. "What do you say, Anne?"

"Oh yes, let's," his wife said. "I haven't played croquet since I was a girl."

Dink smiled beatifically. "That's settled, then. We'll play in teams. I'll be referee."

"Excellent idea." Max unfolded from his chair in a graceful movement. Joining Jenna at the sideboard, he refilled his teacup. "I'll partner Jenna."

Carolyn's smile was chilling. "Has anyone ever noticed," she asked the room at large, "how particularly unattractive a man with a mustache appears when he salivates?"

Max studied his wife for a moment. "At least it's human, darling." He switched his gaze to Jenna. "There are those of us who are attracted to warmth."

"And there are those of us, *darling*, who are attracted to masculinity," Carolyn countered. "I'll partner Ralph. What do you say, Ralph? Shall we show Max and Miss Howard how the game is played?"

Max slung a careless arm around Jenna's waist. "I believe we've been challenged." He dropped his gaze to her lips. "Are you the sort of woman who likes a challenge?"

Jenna stepped forward, dislodging his arm. "*Challenge* sounds so terribly civilized," she said, smiling slightly. "When I play croquet"—she gave the last word special emphasis—"I'm not the least bit civilized. Ralph," she called across the room, "we're going to beat the pants off you."

Everyone laughed, and the tension in the room eased. Soon they were making bets on the winner. As Jenna joked with the others, she felt her competitive spirit rise, and along with it came a momentary, disconcerting dizziness, causing the room to shift sideways before her eyes.

Dammit, she thought violently as perspiration broke out on her palms, why couldn't she even play a simple child's game without going off the deep end?

She had to get away. Maybe she couldn't outrun the weakness in herself, but she certainly didn't need anyone around when she made the attempt. She preferred to fight her battles in private.

Moving away from the sideboard, she walked to the end of the table, where Dink was in the process of finishing off the strawberries.

"You should be playing," Jenna whispered. "It's the perfect chance for you to give your impersonation of Lady Georgiana. You can cheat like hell, and everyone will have to pretend they don't notice."

A light kindled in Dink's eyes. "You're right. They'll—" She broke off and shook her head. "We're playing partners. The numbers will be uneven."

Jenna shrugged. "Hey, what are friends for? I'll pull up a headache so you can partner Max."

"But you won't be able to see me."

"Tell me about it later."

Leaving Dink to make her excuses for her, Jenna walked out of the dining room, down the hall, and out a side door. She didn't slow down until she was a good distance from the castle. She walked in no particular direction. She only wanted to get away, away from people, away from polite conversation, away from the necessity of maintaining a pleasant expression.

Gradually the incredible peace of the countryside began to nudge at her. She felt the soft warmth of the sun on her face and the gentle touch of the breeze in her hair. Almost against her will, her aggressive steps slowed, and her frustrations faded into nothing.

Ireland was a compassionate country, she realized. In every direction she looked, she found only tenderness and tranquillity. There was nothing glaring or harsh to the land. It was a country done in watercolors.

As she topped a small rise, Jenna spotted a huge pile of stones, the same type of stone that had been used to build Aldham Castle. Curiosity pulled her toward the rubble, and she spent the next half hour climbing over it, exploring and dreaming, imagining what the rocks must have been, back in the dim mists of the past when they were still joined together.

Then, as she walked around a small outcropping of the stones, she glanced up, and there was Keith.

He wore a cream, cable-knit wool sweater and brown slacks and was leaning against a block of stone the size of a refrigerator. His face was in profile, his thoughts apparently far away. And judging by his features, they weren't altogether pleasant thoughts.

Seconds later, as though sensing her presence, he turned his head toward her. Instantly the deep creases in his brow disappeared. He seemed surprised to see her, but there was also pleasure in his dark eyes, pleasure and that ever-present gleam of amusement.

"So you've finally come, then?" he said. "And not before time."

A gurgle of laughter escaped her. "Didn't we play this scene yesterday?" she asked, her violet eyes sparkling.

Taking her arm, he proceeded to escort her away from the pile of stones. "Have you ever thought of laughing for a living? You could make a fortune."

She cut her eyes toward him. "*Blarney*'s such a nice, Irish sort of word."

"Are you trying to say I have a flattering

tongue?" He exhaled in an exaggerated martyr's sigh. "Don't you know I would never think to deceive you?"

"But you'll pull my leg every chance you get," Jenna said, her voice stern, her eyes smiling.

He grinned. "You happen to be in possession of two of the most attractive legs I've ever come across. I can't say I would mind pulling either of them."

"Blarney."

He shook his head. "No, and to my way of thinking, that word has fallen on hard times."

"How so?"

"Today people use it to mean insincere flattery, but once, in the past, blarney was a magical thing, a wonderful gift given to a king. You've heard of the Blarney Stone? It's a block of limestone in Blarney Castle, down by Cork. And you've probably heard that anyone who kisses it receives the gift of persuasion, but do you know why?"

She shook her head. "But I have a feeling you're going to tell me."

"Since you ask so nicely, I will. It seems the young king who used to live in Blarney Castle was walking by the river one winter day and—"

"What was his name?"

He glanced at her with frown. "His name?"

"He had to have a name," she pointed out logically. "Irish kings had wonderful names, like Aldfrith and Carbery of the Liffey and Feidlimid—"

"Barney," he said, sounding unaccountably harassed. "His name was Barney."

"Barney of Blarney? It doesn't have quite the same élan as the other—"

"Do you want to hear the story or not?"

"Of course, of course," she said soothingly. "He was walking by the river . . ."

"*As* I was saying, it was in the middle of winter, and no living creature was stirring, which made Barney pay extra attention when he heard the sound, a wild wailing that pierced him to the bones. And there, rising from the water, was a pale, almost fleshless hand. Being a foolishly brave young man, he immediately jumped into the river and pulled on the hand . . . which by chance was attached to the body of an old woman, a witch by trade. To reward him for saving her life, the old woman cast a spell on Barney. All he had to do was kiss one particular stone in Blarney Castle while he was still under the witch's spell and he would forever after have the power of sweet, persuading speech."

He paused to glance at Jenna. "You're probably thinking that it was no big deal, right? Go kiss a rock and poof! instant charisma. But have you ever seen a picture of the Blarney Stone?"

She shook her head. "Is it in the moat or something?"

"No, that would be easy. The stone's located below one of the machicolations in the battlements of the castle. If you want to kiss it, they grab you by the heels and lower you headfirst over the side." He finished with something close to boyish relish.

"How did it feel?" she asked, unperturbed.

"Oh, I haven't done it. My sweet tongue was born yesterday . . . right after I first set eyes on the queen of the fairies," he added just as they reached a pony cart waiting in a narrow lane.

Taking Jenna's elbow, he helped her into the

cart. "That's enough dawdling," he scolded. "We'll have to hurry, or we'll be late."

Jenna stared at the aged horse, then down at the cart. "These are not really yours," she said in disbelief. "The twentieth century has arrived, even in dear, old County Limerick."

He rustled the reins, urging the arthritic animal forward. "It's here, sure enough. And puzzling times they are. I have an automobile, but fuel costs money. Grass is free."

"Tight purse or tight fist?"

He laughed. "I admit I can get more use from a penny that most men, but the truth is, I like the old pony cart. There are no fumes to pollute the air. And no noise to disturb the wee creatures." When she raised one questioning brow, he added, "Don't give me that skeptical look. I'm referring to the birds and small animals. But the best reason for taking the cart is old Donny knows the way. So I can lay down the reins and throw me arm around a cozy lass if I've a mind to."

When he lay the reins at his feet and put one arm around her shoulders, Jenna gazed up at him for a moment, then said, "If you say *faith and begorra* just once, I'm going to punch you."

A corner of his lip twitched slightly. "What's ailing you, lass?"

"You know very well what I'm talking about. You can drop the Hollywood-Irish dialect anytime you want," she said dryly. "You are as American as I am, so quit going all quaint and *Erin go bragh* on me."

He threw back his head and laughed, pulling her close in a brief, warm hug. "I thought you would appreciate a bit of Emerald Isle charm."

"You know what I would really appreciate?"

"What?" he said, studying her features warily.

"I'd appreciate knowing where it is old Donny knows the way to, and why we're in such an all-fired hurry to get there. I feel like Alice, chasing after that twitty little White Rabbit."

He raised one brow in surprise. "We're going to the fair. Didn't I tell you?"

"You know damn well you didn't," she said. But after a moment she shook her head, realizing it didn't matter where they were going.

Smile at me and I'll follow you anywhere, she thought in bemusement.

Jenna knew she was being drawn into the make-believe world and the make-believe sensations of the day before, but suddenly it didn't seem to matter. *It's my vacation,* she told herself. *And if I want to indulge in childish fantasies, that's my business.*

The village of Slyne-Dun-Carrick, roughly five miles from Aldham Castle, was teeming with people. The words *quaint, charming,* and *picturesque* kept popping into her mind. They could have been used to describe the village, the fair, the people, and even the air Jenna was breathing.

As they walked along the cobblestone streets, it seemed that every other person they passed was a close, longtime friend of Keith's, and an unmistakable hint of pride entered his voice as he presented Jenna to each of them.

"I'm never going to remember all the names," she moaned to Keith as they stood in a narrow, crowded street. "What happens when I meet Thomas later and start talking to him, then find out he's really Jamie?"

"It won't matter," he said, his eyes sparkling. "Jamie, Thomas, or Paddy, any of them will answer to anything you like. You've got a way about you, acushla."

He stood staring down at her, and Jenna found herself drawn once again into the warmth she saw in his eyes. She leaned toward him, unable to prevent the slight movement, and watched with dazed, uncomprehending eyes as he dipped his head, his lips drawing closer and closer.

Her breath caught in her throat. Nothing had happened, she told herself. He hadn't even kissed her. But she was seduced. She was seduced by an almost-kiss.

Seconds later, when pedestrians surged around them, pushing them apart, the spell was broken. Keith simply took her hand and began walking beside her again.

After they had browsed at a hectic, picturesque stock show, Keith led Jenna through narrow, charming back streets to a noisy, quaint public house for a drink. The brew they were served was neither picturesque, quaint, nor charming. Stout, as far as Jenna was concerned, deserved its name. As she was struggling to swallow her first mighty mouthful, Keith introduced her to a man whose name Jenna was certain she would have no trouble remembering.

Duffy—if he had a last name, no one seemed to remember it—was Keith's head lad at Donegal Farm. The "lad" was eighty if he was a day. He was a wrinkled, weathered, teak-brown gnome of a man.

"I work for Keith Donegal, as I did for his father and his father's father," Duffy told her when Keith moved away to speak to Jamie, Thomas, or Paddy.

Jenna narrowed her eyes at the gnarled old man. "No one is that old," she said, her voice blunt.

Duffy rubbed his chin but didn't manage to hide the twinkle in his milky gray eyes. "Well, I might have exaggerated a bit, but it's truth that I've been on Donegal Farm since before I had sense enough to know it. I was born there, you see. My father worked for Keith's grandfather."

"I can't imagine staying at one place for an entire lifetime," she said, her voice slightly wistful.

"You'll find there's not an abundance of change around here. We labor at the same task through every day and go for a pint at the same pub every night." He leaned his elbows on the table. "Here's how it happened. The good God was up in heaven, making His plans, and He got to thinkin' what would make the perfect life here on earth. Well, as He looked around Him, there in the immediate area of heaven, He thought what a lovely place it was and wasn't it a shame the poor mortals on earth didn't have anything so wonderful. With pity in His heart, He threw down a piece of heaven, and it landed— you'll not guess where—it landed in Ireland. That's right, right here in our own County Limerick."

Jenna considered his words for a moment, then nodded. "I'll accept that." When he gave a cracked, rattling laugh, she added, "But you say there's *never* change?"

"Change? No, we like it just fine as we have it." His dark face crinkled in a smile. "But that's not to say we don't like a bit of surprise now and then, just to make a good life sparkle, you see."

As she laughed in delight, Duffy studied her

face. Then after a moment he said, "I'm thinking you'll do, all right. Our Keith hasn't had a good life, but he's a good man for all that. He's paid dear for the happiness that's ahead, but looking at you, I can see you were well worth the waiting."

Jenna frowned. "Why did you say that? Duffy, what's—"

But the old man was already moving across the crowded room with a friend who had hailed him earlier.

Slowly Jenna turned her head toward where Keith stood at the bar with three other men. Yesterday, when he had found her on the rocky ledge, Keith had said something similar. And he had never really explained what he had meant.

Something was going on, Jenna thought as she caught her lower lip between her teeth. She had thought Keith was giving her some kind of come-on. A quaint, charming, picturesque, Irish come-on. Now she didn't know what to think.

Rising to her feet, she made her way toward Keith, but, as though events had been carefully orchestrated, half a dozen newcomers chose that moment to enter the pub, and during the ensuing introductions, Jenna was drawn into a vigorous discussion, and the opportunity for questions was lost.

It was almost one o'clock before Jenna remembered she had left the castle without telling Dink. "Keith!" She stood on tiptoes and shouted in his general direction. "I need a telephone."

With gestures and more shouting she finally made him understand, and he guided her out of the pub, down more narrow back streets, and into a small square, where she found a telephone kiosk.

"Dink?" Jenna said as soon as her friend came on the line. "I just thought I'd better let you know that I'm not in my room resting."

"I may be slow, but I did figure that out," Dink said, her voice dry. "Where are you? I thought maybe you'd fallen victim to some Irish long-leggedy beastie . . . or maybe the ghost of poor, depraved Uncle Edward."

Jenna glanced at Keith and smiled. "Not quite," she told Dink. "I'm at the fair."

"Ahhh, it's the Brigadoon man again."

"The one and only," Jenna confirmed. "If I'm not back in a couple of days, call Gene Kelly and tell him to come find me, " she added before replacing the receiver.

"You know Gene Kelly?" Keith asked as she hung up the receiver. "Does he live in Dallas?"

"No, I—" She broke off when she saw the laughter in his eyes. "How would you like a thick ear? It'll be a nice match for your head."

He laughed. "How would you like some lunch?" he countered. "Are you hungry?"

"Starving," she said emphatically.

Although Jenna had exaggerated, she was hungry, and that surprised her. She hadn't had an appetite in weeks, months really. And now that her body seemed to be coming out of hibernation, she was ready to make up for lost time.

The fair offered dozens of choices for an appetite that had been in cold storage. Jenna wasn't a shy woman, and she changed her mind a dozen times before Keith, in exasperation, bought meat pies, fruit, and great chunks of cake, which he stored in the pony cart.

An hour later they had finished their lunch and sat side-by-side on a misty purple blanket that was spread on the bank of a wide, shallow river. Towering trees grew close to the river and leaned toward one another to form an arch. The rays of the afternoon sun filtering through the branches, the patches of yellow and green and blue gleaming brilliantly, the branches soaring up above—all combined to create Nature's cathedral.

Beside her, Keith tossed a pebble into the river, disturbing crystal-clear water sliding over the rocks in the riverbed. "I come here as often as I can so the water can talk to me," he said with a slight smile. "The water tells me where it's been and about all the sights it's seen."

"You ever get around to discussing politics?" she asked lazily.

"I discuss. And the water always agrees with me." He inhaled deeply, glancing at her. "I do like it here. At times I think Ireland is the best place on earth." He glanced away from her. "There have been other places, exciting places, which all seemed best at the time."

"But you didn't choose any of those places."

"I didn't. I couldn't. At night, while I lay sleeping, Erin called to me. So I came back to Donegal Farm." He drew in a slow breath. "Four generations of Donegals have lived in that house, and the land has been ours for longer than memory can hold."

"I envy you," she said softly. "I know nothing about my ancestors—who they were, where they came from. I have three living grandparents, two on Mother's side and one on Daddy's, but they don't live close, so I see them only on the occasional holiday. I've never sat down and talked to them, really talked to them, about their parents and grandparents, about their memories."

"No brothers or sisters?"

She shook her head. "There was a baby boy, but he died before I was born. I always wondered if it would have been different if he had lived." She paused. "We're not a close family. I've never understood my parents, and they've never understood me. I'm afraid I'm a big disappointment to them."

"No, you have that wrong," he said with quiet assurance. "That's impossible."

The sincerity in his face produced an uncomfortable constriction in her throat and chest. "You don't know," she said ruefully. "I've disappointed a lot of people over the years. My parents, teachers . . . my ex-fiancé."

"Ah, an ex-fiancé. I don't think I like the sound of him."

She smiled. "Greg was just a nice, ordinary man. Very intelligent actually. But he wanted me to be something I couldn't be. Greg thought art served no useful purpose in life. He wanted me to be a corporate wife." She glanced at him. "You've known me for two days, what kind of corporate wide do you think I would make?"

His expression was quizzical as he studied her. Then he said, "If you were crazy enough to marry a corporation in the first place, I think you would be a good wife to it. But what kind of children would you have?"

She giggled. "Adorable little pink-and-blue subsidiaries. No, you know what I mean. I can't be structured. I try to say and do the 'correct' thing, but words are always coming out of my mouth before I can stop them."

"I think you'll do just fine without the fiancé," he said firmly, "but parents are a different thing. Why do you say you disappointed them?"

She shrugged helplessly. "They wanted me to be a lawyer and join the family practice. They're both attorneys. Very successful attorneys." She paused. "Success is important to my parents. I don't suppose either of them knew how much it hurt knowing I couldn't be what they wanted. They simply couldn't see that even if I had studied law, I wouldn't have been any good at it."

She thought about those years, the emotional turmoil, the self-doubt. She had wanted so badly for her parents to be proud of her. She had desperately needed them to be pleased that she was their daughter. Back then the need for her parents' approval had been the driving force in her life. It was the reason she had dropped out of college, the reason she had turned down the art scholarship that would have allowed her to study in Paris. Because Jenna had known that it would have been years, maybe even decades, before she received any real recognition as a serious artist.

"I might never have gotten there," she murmured aloud, then shook her head. "It's better this way. I've shown them that I can be a success at something."

"And they're proud as punch of you?"

She gave a short laugh. "They tease me a little about my work being shown in some of the best bathrooms in the country. But, yes, I suppose they're glad I'm successful. I don't see them all that much."

"Queen Brianna," he said, his eyes trained on a spot across the river.

"I beg your pardon."

He shook his head and smiled. "It's just a story someone told me a long time ago, a story with a not very subtle moral, I'm afraid."

"One of those," she said with a grimace. "Did it teach you a valuable lesson?"

His laugh was slightly rough. "Let's just say the jury's still out on that one."

"Tell me the story and I'll decide."

He cut his eyes toward her and smiled. "Using your vast store of knowledge concerning Keith Donegal?" He shrugged. "Why not? You're an American, therefore intrinsically in need of a moral tale. Calm down," he said, laughing at her huff of indignation. "I'm teasing.

"The story is all about a fairy queen who, by a strange coincidence, happened to look a lot like you. Hair black as soot, skin the color of fresh, sweet cream," he murmured as he ran his gaze over her face, "and no bigger than could stand on the palm of your hand. Brianna was her name. Sometimes she appeared as a mortal, so lovely that all who saw her fell instantly in love. But mostly she stayed among the other fairies, and then she wore her wings, wings that were shot through with pure gold. If you were quiet and very lucky, you might see her flying about, a golden aura surrounding her. Even the other fairies, who are all pretty spectacular creatures, caught their breath at the sight of her.

"Then one day, as she was flying near a branch of this very river, Queen Brianna met her fate."

It was a fairy tale, Jenna told herself. A story to

tell sleepy children. Logically she knew that, but some nuance in Keith's voice, some flash of feeling in his dark eyes, had brought a fine tension into the air between them, as though the words had a different, deeper meaning.

She cleared her throat. "I've always wondered what fate looked like."

His smile was slightly twisted. "I imagine fate takes different shapes for different people, but in this case it came in the guise of a young fairy prince. He had a fine, elegant face, and his clothes were made of the dawn sky. On his feet were little pink shoes that turned up at the toes."

"Pink shoes?" Jenna repeated doubtfully. "Are you sure they were pink?"

"His shoes were pink," he said emphatically. "You might have grave doubts concerning his masculinity, but to a fairy queen he was top of the line. When Brianna saw him, love struck deep in her heart, but what she didn't know was that although the young man was as handsome as could be, he was also moody and insincere, the superficial type who is never satisfied with anything."

"I think I met him at a barbecue once."

Firmly ignoring her, he went on with the tale. "Unfortunately this beautiful fellow didn't love Brianna in return, and he wasn't at all impressed by her golden wings. No, he spent all his time admiring the birds, especially the bluebirds. He would sigh and clasp a hand to his heart whenever he saw the blue wings fluttering about him, and no matter what Brianna did, she couldn't make him take notice of her. He could see only the blue wings of the birds.

"Brianna grew desperate, and one day when a spring rain cloud formed in the sky, she decided to fly through the cloud, hoping it would color her wings blue so that her young man would notice her. As she flew through again and again, her wings began to take on the color of the cloud. But of course every time she gained a bit of the false color, she lost some of the true."

He paused. "And that's why to this day, in spring at sunset, behind the blue rain clouds, you can see a golden aura at the edge of the clouds."

Jenna stared at him silently for a moment. "You left something out. Or is this one of those write-your-own-ending kind of things?"

He laughed. "No, there's an ending, but since it's pretty pitiful, I wasn't sure you wanted to hear it."

"Lay it on me, I can take it."

Picking up another pebble, he tossed it into the water and said, "Queen Brianna got her wish. The young fairy prince fell in love with her, but being the kind of man he was, it didn't last long. After a while he decided he preferred red wings. Heartbroken, Brianna went home, back to the people who had loved her all her life. But to her dismay, she found that her family and friends no longer recognized her. To them she was simply an ordinary fairy with ordinary blue wings."

Giving an inelegant snort, Jenna rolled her eyes. "You were right. That's a pitiful ending. You know what I think? I think if you're dumb enough to fall for a man wearing pink shoes, you get what you deserve."

He laughed. "The story wasn't about pink shoes." Then, glancing down at his hands, he added. "The point is, you've got to be what you are. Anything else diminishes you."

As silence fell between them, she studied his face in profile. She had been right. Something about the story was affecting him deeply.

"Okay, the jury's in," she said abruptly. "I think the guy with the pink shoes wasn't the only silly one in that story. Brianna made a judgment call and she screwed up, but blue wings or gold, she was still Brianna, and her fellow fairies were a bunch of dimwits not to see that."

When he went very still, she was afraid she had said the wrong thing, but after a moment he turned toward her and slowly, carefully closed the small gap between them.

It wasn't the first time Jenna had been kissed. In fact there had been quite a few kisses in her past. There had been sweet, tentative kisses and wildly passionate kisses. But at the first touch of Keith's mouth, all memory of the other kisses vanished, canceled by a more powerful force.

The moment his strong lips began to move on hers, Jenna recognized that something strange and wonderful was happening. All the hurts, all the anger and fear that she kept hidden away, began to loosen. It was as though giant, painful knots that had been stored away in her soul were being suddenly, gently untied. On Keith's lips she tasted healing. She tasted freedom.

As he pressed her back on the blanket, she felt his heartbeat join hers. It was like nothing else she had ever experienced. For a moment—for just an instant—she felt that every muscle in his arms and chest, every beat of his heart belonged to her.

But then the depth of her response began to disturb her. It was too much, too soon, Jenna told herself. She didn't trust the feeling. She had spent too many years with her bonds, and being without them, even momentarily, was unfamiliar and even a little frightening.

In a panicky reaction she pulled her lips away from his. Ignoring the sudden sense of loss, she sat up and smoothed her hair back with a trembling hand.

"I—" She broke off and cleared her throat. "That was very nice."

She shot a glance at him, and when she saw the fire in his eyes, the confusion in his frown, she allowed a breath of relief to escape. She wasn't the only one who had been moved.

"Very nice," he echoed, his voice rough, almost hard, "if you like volcano eruptions." In the next moment the frown became a smile. "And apparently I do."

She studied his lean features. "Keith, what did Duffy mean when he said I was worth waiting for?"

The silence following her question was so lengthy, she was afraid he wasn't going to answer at all. Then he sat up and rested his hands on his drawn-up knees.

"I was born late in my father's life," he said. "I still can't understand why he married my mother. They were . . . totally unsuited. Divorcing was the most sensible thing they did together. I—"

He broke off, and cleared his throat. "Suffice it to say, I disappointed him as well, especially after my mother and I went to the United States to live. There were so many things he expected from a son. So many things."

Giving his head a sharp shake, he said, "But I'm getting away from your question. You see, Da had a great wish. He wanted to see his grandchildren before he died. I wanted to give him that, Jenna. I can't tell you how much I wanted it. And there were a few women who would have taken on the job of being my wife."

Looking at him, Jenna knew there were probably a good many women who would have taken on the job. Eagerly and with great haste.

"But you didn't marry," she said quietly.

"I couldn't marry. Da understood that. He agreed that I couldn't possibly marry any of those women."

She frowned her bewilderment. "Why? Why couldn't you marry?"

"Because none of them was right."

Rising to his feet, he reached down to help her up, and in his eyes there was something she couldn't identify, something that made her shiver.

"None of them were you," he said, his voice flat and matter-of-fact.

Dumbfounded, Jenna searched for a response, but found nothing. This was right out of her territory. If she had been in Dallas, and if she had been with an ordinary man, she would have been wary of those quietly spoken words. She would have written Keith off as a too-intense Romeo and gotten away from him as quickly as possible.

But Jenna wasn't in Dallas, she reminded herself as they gathered up the remains of their picnic and walked back to the pony cart. She was in Ireland. Land of fairies and elves and leprechauns. Mysterious, magical things lurked around every corner. And the man beside her was definitely not an ordinary man. He was part of the magic.

Four

Four

According to Keith, any gathering of Irishmen, no matter how small, was an excuse for a horse race. The fair at Slyne-Dun-Carrick was no exception.

As Jenna watched and absorbed the activity around her, she gradually came to understand that the race wasn't merely a form of entertainment. Everyone, old or young, spectator or participant, threw their whole hearts into the race. Emotions ran high, and excitement crackled in the air. Each conversation contained a volatile element, and the people involved were never sure whether anger or laughter would surface first.

"I thought you raised sheep," Jenna said as Keith finished his inspection of a gleaming brown horse that occasionally tossed its head in regal indifference.

Queen Mab had been transported to the village in a sleek, modern trailer by Duffy and a diminutive young man named Peter who was Duffy's assistant and Keith's jockey. He wore a scarf tied around his upper right arm, a green scarf for the luck of the shamrock.

"Why do you make that sound like an accusation?" Keith asked, giving her a slow smile. "Is there any reason I can't have both?"

"No, but you have to admit this horse doesn't exactly go with the simple-shepherd image. When do we go to the racetrack?"

He glanced to the right, then to the left before returning his gaze to her. "We're there."

She dropped her gaze to the cobblestone beneath her feet. "Here?"

"Right here."

"How quaint and charming and picturesque . . . not to mention messy," she murmured.

He grinned. "It starts here, makes a loop through the countryside, and finishes here." He grabbed her hand. "Come on. They'll be starting any minute."

He began to make his way through the crowd, pulling her along behind him, then they were running down a narrow back street. Minutes later they reached a dirt road at the edge of the village.

Grasping her waist with both hands, Keith lifted her to sit on a low rock wall. "Now we're right by the backstretch," he said as he hopped up beside her.

Only a few minutes had passed before they heard the shouts that meant the race had begun. The rock wall was now lined with eager spectators. Across a field Jenna could see clusters of people gathered along the lane that circled around to where she and Keith waited.

As the horses swung around the bend and came into sight, the crowd around them came to life, shouting encouragement and good-natured threats to the personal favorite of each.

"Where is Mab?" Jenna shouted. "I don't see her. No, wait—there she is!" she said as she spotted Peter's green scarf fluttering in the wind.

Queen Mab seemed to be running level with three other horses, but as they drew nearer, Jenna saw that Keith's horse was holding steady in fourth place.

"*Come on, Mab!*" Jenna screamed, excitement adding strength to her voice. "Keep going, darling, put your heart into it!"

The horse flashed by, and just before they disappeared from sight, Jenna saw Queen Mab pass one of the horses, drawing closer and closer to the two lead horses. And then they disappeared into the village.

From that point on, the race was reported to them by the distant shouts of the spectators, the noise growing louder as the horses made their way back to the starting point.

Moments later a boy standing on a rooftop cupped his hands to his mouth and called out, "Spinner first, Queen Mab second, Riley Boy is third!"

Jenna turned to Keith. "Second! That's wonderful!"

"Not a bad go," he admitted, smiling. "A decent run for her first try. She'll be a winner next time." He helped Jenna down from the wall. "It seems you've brought me luck."

"Where are we going now?" she asked as they began to follow the crowd.

"Back to the pub of course. It's a good time of day. Time to boast and collect money that's owed me. Yes, a very good time of day," he said, drawing in a deep, expansive breath.

"More pennies for you to squeeze?" she teased.

"I shouldn't wonder at it," he said with a grin. "And after that, if you like, some friends have asked us to share their supper."

She liked. In fact Jenna liked everything she had seen and experienced in their day together. But only now did she discover in herself a need to see Keith's friends, to observe him in his natural environment, to watch him interact with people who cared about him.

The soft darkness of a spring evening had spread through the village by the time Jenna stood in a brightly lit kitchen beside Sara Flaherty, wife to Michael Flaherty, Keith's closest friend. Jenna and Sara took care of the dinner dishes as Keith and Michael carried on a conversation that was constantly being interrupted by the Flahertys' four children.

Jenna found her attention returning again and again to Keith. She couldn't seem to keep her eyes off him. She liked his slow smile and the way he squinted his droopy eyes when he lit his pipe. She liked the gentle, caring way he dealt with the children. When she saw his strong, lean fingers tying five-year-old Anna's hair ribbon, Jenna felt pride swell and grow in her chest, bringing a lump to her throat.

For heaven's sake, get a grip. You're going off the deep end, she warned herself. *You don't know this man.*

She had met Keith yesterday. It was no business of hers what kind of man he was. There was no reason for her to feel such ungovernable glory in a man she had only met.

"You won't find a man more highly regarded, more loved, than our Keith there."

Sara's soft words broke into Jenna's thoughts, bringing her gaze back to the tall woman beside her.

"No man works harder," Sara continued. "And the Donegals have always had money. He could well hire people to do the work he does. When he came back, that's what everyone expected of him." She frowned. "Mind you, it's not for that—the money, I mean—that people respect him. He could be penniless and he would still draw people to him. And you can see for yourself how he is with the young folk."

Jenna hid a rueful smile. An Irish yenta. Sara, thoroughly sweet woman that she was, was hauling out Keith's references—lovely man, kind to children, hard worker, well respected, able to support a wife.

"Sara, Keith and I met only yesterday," Jenna explained, stubbornly contradicting her earlier thoughts. "We're not even friends. Not really. We're barely acquaintances."

"You're more than that," Sara said firmly as she dried her hands on her apron. "You may have met only yesterday, but there are times it happens just that way. Take me and Michael. Wasn't I all set to marry Davy Wellan? I hadn't told Davy, mind. But I had it in my head that we were going to marry. Davy was a right-thinking, decent sort of man who would make an agreeable husband for me and a good father to the children I was wantin'. Then what happened but Michael Flaherty came home from his travels in Africa. Then and there he put an end to all my practical thinking. I looked at him and I knew. He didn't have a job, my family didn't think much of him, and he had done some hard living over in Africa—it showed in his eyes. And me, well, you can see for yourself I'm no catch. I didn't have much to bring to a marriage, no money, not even the kind of looks that go down easy."

"But you're beautiful," Jenna protested. "I was thinking earlier how . . . how you sort of glow."

Sara laughed. "You're seeing the love shining out of me. Michael saw it too. He still sees it . . . and thinks it's beauty, poor, daft man. And I saw the same in him. There was no doubt for either of us. Our people got themselves all in a bother, but we're that hardheaded." Her lips curved up in a lovely, confident smile. "After Tim, our third, was born our families decided we were serious about this thing and came around."

"It's a beautiful story," Jenna said slowly, "and you and your husband are a beautiful couple, but you've known Michael all your life. It's different for me. I'm a stranger in a strange land. I don't belong here, and—"

"Don't you?" Sara asked as she studied Jenna's face. "Do you truly feel yourself to be a stranger when you're with Keith Donegal?"

Jenna frowned. "Maybe not, but instant empathy happens all the time. It's not . . . well, *magical* to find mutual understanding with a person you've just met."

"Why do you use that word? Why are you talking about magic?"

Jenna laughed in confusion. "I don't know . . .

it's silly. It's just that sometimes I feel like I've crossed some kind of boundary. Like I'm not in the real world anymore. I guess it's because Ireland is so different from what I'm used to. The castle, the village, Donegal Farm—they all seem like something out of a storybook."

Sara glanced away from her and nodded. "That would explain it, then. I guess I would feel the same if ever I visited America." Turning back to her, the woman smiled. "We have a job now. We have to get all this heathen bunch ready for the street dance."

Sara's assurance should have made Jenna feel easier, but there was something in the other woman's expression that made Jenna want to say, *What is it? What's going on that everyone knows except me?* But Jenna didn't ask. She didn't ask because at some point in the day she realized she wasn't ready to hear the answer.

When they left Sara and Michael's house, Jenna found that the enthusiastic fair-goers, who had been spread throughout the village earlier in the day, were now compressed into a three-block length of the main street for the dance that was to be the climax of the fair.

At each end of the street a makeshift stage had been set up for two very different groups of musicians. At the north end the area youth were catered to. The music wasn't exactly hard rock, but it was lively, sometimes even rowdy. At the south end old tunes were played, tunes that took the more mature revelers back to the days of their own youth.

Jenna and Keith moved back and forth between the unstructured dances of the north end to the more organized reels of the south end. And wherever they happened to be, Jenna's presence was accepted without question. The men who asked her to dance teased her with gentle indulgence, as though she were a much-loved younger sister, and the women treated her with easy familiarity, as though she were a neighbor with whom they were in the habit of gossiping.

When she had finished a whirling dance with Thomas or Jamie or Paddy—she still wasn't sure which was which—Keith caught her by the hand and pulled her away from the crowd to stand next to the stone wall of the general store and post office.

"They've had enough," he said. "The next thousand dances belong to me."

"Thousand?" she repeated, her face flushed with pleasure and exertion. "I may have to change my shoes."

"I've brought you some sustenance." Keith pushed a drink into her hand. "I suppose I should make a toast? To your health? To your beauty? Or maybe to the quaint, charming, picturesque Wee Folk who were kind enough to get into your head and bring you straight to Ireland."

Shaking her head, she said, "We need something with more . . . more grandeur." She raised her glass high. *"Vedi Napoli e poi mori!"*

"See Naples and die? What kind of toast is that to make in County Limerick?"

"Only Latin would do, and it's the only Latin I know," she explained as she turned up her drink and took half of it in one swallow. Instantly heat flooded her face, and she leaned against the wall for support as she went through a coughing fit.

"Sweet saints in heaven," she wheezed, gasping for breath. "What is this stuff? Drinking horse liniment is some quaint Irish custom, right?"

Laughing, Keith stopped pounding her on the back and took the glass from her hand. "Haven't you ever wondered why Irishmen are big and strong and a bit off their beam? Here's your answer." He tossed down his drink. "Good Irish whiskey, distilled in Francis Mulrooney's cow shed."

It was Jenna's first taste of home-brewed whiskey, but unfortunately it wasn't to be her last. Well-meaning, hospitable friends kept pressing more on her, and because she didn't want to hurt anyone's feelings, she accepted each drink. She disposed of quite a bit of it in alleys and trash cans, but there always seemed to be someone there to give her another one. As a result she soon made the gratifying discovery that she was an authority on Irish country dances.

"I'm really good at this," she shouted to Keith as he whirled her around.

His lips twitched uncontrollably, and he whirled her again. "You're a lovely dancer."

"One thing, Keith? she yelled.

"What's that, alanna?"

"Why didn't I see all the strobe lights when we first got here?"

When he pulled her into his arms, she could feel his body shaking with laughter. "Because they're only for us. Magic lights, found only in a bottle and in your eyes."

"It's better than any disco in Dallas," she said earnestly, then swung away from him. As she moved, her feet automatically kept time with the music.

"Jenna?" he said, grabbing her hand.

"I like this step. Here, watch this." She shot a glance at him. "How's that for someone who's never done a jig in her life?"

"It was wonderful," he admitted. "But there's one thing I feel I should tell you."

"What?" Her voice was distracted as she spun away from him, then back.

"The music has stopped."

Her steps slowed. "Oh? When?"

"About two minutes ago."

She glanced around, then smiled and waved as the group of people around them began to laugh and applaud.

"Thank you, thank you," she said, dipping in an unsteady curtsy. "You're too kind." She glanced at Keith. "Should I take it on the road? You know that old saying: 'But will it play in Slyne-Dun-Carrick?'"

He stared down at her, holding her loosely in the circle of his arms. "You're a wonder," he said softly, shaking his head. "Such a small woman. Such a miracle of a woman."

"I wasn't *that* good."

He chuckled. "Time for coffee."

"Irish coffee?" she asked hopefully.

"No, straight and black and strong."

"Party pooper."

When he left her to fetch the coffee, Jenna moved to lean against a nearby wall, savoring the warm glow that enveloped her tonight. The fact that the glow had a slight alcoholic content didn't bother her in the least. She knew the whiskey had merely relaxed her so that she could better appreciate the warmth.

A short while later, as she was humming a tune under her breath, Jenna noticed a woman who had moved to stand beside her. She was a tall woman, in her late fifties or early sixties, and her salt-and-pepper hair had been pulled straight back from her thin, unlined face. She was not a pretty woman, but her features were attractive in a stern, unbending way.

Jenna's lips twitched in a smile of greeting, but gradually the smile faded. All day Jenna had been treated with open warmth and acceptance by Keith's friends and neighbors. It was a shock when she recognized the undisguised animosity in this woman's narrowed eyes.

"We haven't met," the woman said abruptly. "I'm Fiona Blair."

Jenna extended her hand. "Hello, I'm—"

"I've known Keith since the day he was born," she said, the words clipped and harsh as she ignored both Jenna's hand and her greeting. "His mother was my best friend."

"How nice," Jenna murmured, feeling increasingly more uncomfortable.

"When are you going back to America?"

"My plans are flexible. Two weeks, maybe three."

"That's too long." Fiona glanced away from Jenna. When she spotted Keith making his way toward them through the crowd, her lips tightened into a thin, pale, disapproving line. "You'll hurt him. You're not the one, and that's sure. Have you lived on a farm? Have you done the hard work that a farmer's wife does each and every day of her life? Do you know anything about making a man like him happy? I'll tell you this: You are the wrong one."

Jenna knew immediately how she should respond. She should tell Fiona that she would never be a farmer's wife so the question was irrelevant. She should say that since she and Keith barely knew each other, Fiona's objections were not only premature, they were downright silly.

But Jenna had a thing about intimidation. It always lit a fire under her obstinacy. With a small, tight smile she said, "Don't you think Keith should be the one to decide whether or not I'm wrong for him?"

Fiona Blair studied her, her lips tight with unconcealed contempt. "He's only a man, and men make mistakes. He may be drawn to the sound of America in you, but *you are not the one*," the woman finished in a harsh whisper. Then she turned away and disappeared into the crowd.

A frosty breeze swirled down the street, surrounding Jenna, almost as though it had sought her out, and bringing a shiver to her spine.

The whole scene reminded her of something from a Disney movie—the mysterious evil queen appearing with a cold wind and a clap of thunder, chilling everything and everyone in the area. But this time the coldness was only for Jenna.

She was still staring at the spot where Fiona had stood when Keith returned with the coffee.

She wasn't sure if it was the warmth of the coffee—he brought two cups and insisted she drink them both—or Keith's presence, but the chill Fiona Blair had left behind disappeared instantly, making her wonder if she had imagined the whole incident.

"Is that real music?" she asked as she became aware of a beautiful melody in the air.

"A waltz." Removing the coffee cup from her hand, he said, "Will you waltz with me, Jenna?"

She went into his arms, closed her eyes, and gave herself over to the music.

"Why are you smiling like that?"

"Because I feel another Disney spell coming on," she said, keeping her eyes closed.

"Dizzy? It's the whiskey."

She laughed and shook her head without explaining. She was relaxed, but not relaxed enough to tell him that she had become Cinderella moving around the grand ballroom in the arms of her Prince Charming. A spotlight followed their movements, and the people around them faded into the shadows as the man with her, this Prince of Charm, looked down at her with a world of love in his eyes.

But then the music stopped, and her eyes opened. There was no ballroom, no spotlight. She was on a village street filled with people, and the man who held her had eyes that were shining with laughter, urging her to share the fun.

A moment later he took her hand and led her through the crowd, away from the lights and music, toward the pony cart. As they walked, Jenna found herself caught up in some in-between world, half of her still given over to the sweet sensations she had felt in his arms while the other half had returned to reality.

On the ride home the fantasy of the night began to slide away from her, moving just beyond her reach. When she recognized what was happening, she fought against it. She wasn't ready for the night to end, not yet.

"Let's go hunting," she said as they pulled up to the front door of the castle. "Let's do it, Keith. Let's go find some leprechauns."

"You don't believe in leprechauns." His voice was as soft and dark as the night.

"Tonight I do. Tonight the enchantment is in me."

"Tonight the whiskey is in you. You need more coffee."

She groaned. "No more coffee. My eyes were blue before you started pouring that stuff down me."

"Not blue," he said in a husky whisper. "Deep violet. The color of the foxgloves in the hazelnut grove behind the house. Sometimes when I stop and push the leaves and grass aside, I see them looking up at me. Like they've been there forever, hiding their beauty from everyone, just waiting until I came along to find them."

With the last word he lowered his head and brushed his lips against hers, once, twice, and then she was in his arms, and the kiss became more solid, more sustaining. In his arms she flowed with feeling. In his arms she almost found the emphatic security she had dreamed of as a child.

Almost, but not quite. She needed to be held tighter, with more vehemence. She needed him to enfold her, to shield her, to hide her from the rest of the world. She wanted him to hold her so close that she wouldn't be able to distinguish his heartbeat from her own. She wanted . . . She wanted . . .

"Come with me," she whispered against his strong lips.

Suddenly he was holding her away from him, his fingers digging painfully into her shoulders. "Do you think you would ask me the same thing tomorrow, when you're stone-cold sober?"

His voice was different, harder now, and the difference made Jenna strain to see his features through the darkness. At that moment the clouds moved, and the moon's light caught the dark eyes of the man with her.

She didn't recognize him. This was not the man she had danced with only a half hour ago. This was not the gentle shepherd who had given her tea and comfort in his kitchen. This was a stranger, whose harsh features made her catch her breath in surprise and alarm.

"When you're not full of enchantment," he said, his voice almost conversational, "will you still want me to make love to you Jenna?"

She moistened her lips, confused now. "I don't know," she whispered.

As she watched, she saw him shake free of the disquieting mood. "That's what I was afraid of." His eyes were gentle again as he drew in a slow breath. "Maybe we'd better wait until you know."

Moments later she was at the door of the castle, still swaying from passion and whiskey and bewilderment as she watched the pony cart and the gentle, disturbing man disappear into the night.

Five

Pausing at the top of the stairs, Jenna winced at the bright morning sunlight that was filtering through the small windows set high in stone walls. After a moment she placed a steadying hand on the balustrade and, taking a deep breath for courage, she prepared to descend.

This was not going to be fun, she told herself. Her head was not quite attached this morning and she was pretty sure any sudden movement would jar it loose.

Seconds later, when she heard footsteps in the hall behind her, Jenna knew immediately that Carolyn Glendening-Waite was about to appear. It was that kind of day. But unless Jenna wanted to leave her head behind, she couldn't run. There was nothing she could do but brave it out.

Jenna had taken one cautious step downward when the redhead joined her on the stairs, looking as though she had just stepped out of Elizabeth Arden's salon.

The woman took a moment to run her gaze over Jenna, frowning like an army sergeant inspecting a raw recruit, which is exactly what Jenna felt like. Her red sweater and gray culottes had looked passable in her bedroom mirror, and she knew her hair, drawn to the back of her neck with a red clip, was relatively neat, but under Carolyn's ruthless gaze, Jenna felt like something pulled from the bottom of a rag bag.

"You look a bit rough, dear," Carolyn said, satisfaction sparkling in her eyes. "Georgiana told us you were trying your hand at mixing with the locals last evening, but if I were you, I would be careful. Outsiders are never truly accepted in this part of the country. The villagers make a great show of being friendly, and then they call you a silly outlander behind your back."

She paused to let her point sink in. "Country fairs are amusing, but it's best to keep your distance. To avoid misunderstandings on both sides, you understand."

Although Jenna's brain wasn't working at full speed, she was pretty sure this woman wouldn't give a damn if she were drawn and quartered by the "locals." Carolyn wanted a confrontation, that much was obvious, and at any other time Jenna would have readily taken her on. But not today. Today Jenna recognized in herself the overpowering urge to whine.

"It's nice of you to take the time to worry about me," Jenna said, flinching as the sound of her own words reverberated through the empty, raw chambers of her skull. "Breakfast," she added weakly. "Everyone will be waiting."

"Not for me. I'm going out." Brushing against

Jenna's shoulder as she passed, Carolyn began pulling on white gloves and ran lightly down the stairs. Without looking back, she called, "Tell Georgiana I may be back late."

Jenna wasn't sure she could manage a curtsy, so she simply said, "Yes, ma'am."

In the dining room Jenna found that the only people sitting at the breakfast table were Dink and the children.

The former blinked twice in an exaggerated stare as Jenna walked into the room. "What are you doing up? I figured you would sleep the day away."

Jenna's only answer was to go to the sideboard and pour a cup of coffee with an unsteady hand as she kept her gaze carefully away from the food.

"Aunt Jenna, you look just like Squeaky."

Jeff's piercing voice made Jenna flinch and spill coffee on her hand. Turning slowly, she pinned the boy with a narrow-eyed gaze. "How old are you?"

"Six."

"If you want to live to see seven"—her voice was soft and slow—"Squeaky had better not be anything reptilian."

Amelia squealed with laughter, causing Jenna to catch her breath in pain. "Squeaky's a rabbit," the four-year-old said. "He has pink eyes, and his nose does like this." She put her finger to her nose to make it wiggle.

Jenna stared at the children for a moment before cutting her gaze sharply toward Dink. "I agreed to visit you. I agreed to be awed and envious. I agreed to call you Lady Geogiana and let you look down your nose at me for being a commoner. I did *not* agree to let your sadistic children take potshots at me first thing in the morning."

Dink shrugged callously. "Serves you right for drinking too much of the good Irish brew."

"How do you know I drank too much?" Jenna asked as she sat down next to her friend.

"You don't get Squeaky eyes from Hawaiian Punch." Dink took a maliciously enthusiastic bite of scrambled eggs. "How was the Brigadoon man?"

Jenna raised her cup and took a long sip of coffee, sighing in relief as the caffeine hit her system. "As far as I'm concerned he just disappeared into the mist for another hundred years."

Dink laughed. "Poor Jenna. You must have been *really* bad last night. Why punish the darling man because of your likin' of a drop or two?"

"Or three or four," Jenna said with listless self-contempt. "The darling man let me drink that lethal stuff." She closed her eyes, trying to shut out the memory of the night before. It didn't work. "He let me make a fool of myself, Dink."

Her friend clapped her hands in childish glee. I knew coming here would be good for you."

Jenna raised her head slowly and stared at the woman beside her for a long, intense moment. "Why do I like you?"

"Because I'm the only person you know who's shorter than you are. I make you feel powerful."

"You make feel like running for cover," Jenna amended, eyeing Dink cautiously. "You're a very strange person. I can't think how you came to be my friend. And how on earth did someone like Geoffrey, who seems reasonably sane, get hooked up with you?"

Dink rubbed her swollen belly with smug assurance. "I'm Geoffrey's salvation. Without me he would turn into a stuffy old man." As she studied Jenna's face, Dink's expression changed, growing serious. "I want things for you, Jenna. I want you to have the kind of happiness I've found. I want you to live, *really* live, your own life."

"Whose have I been living?" she asked acidly, then after a small sigh, relented. "People have to find fulfillment in their own way. I don't think my future includes being some poor man's salvation."

"No," Dink agreed. "But he might be yours. I worry about you. Unless you're unattractive or a nun or one of *those* women, you shouldn't be a V-I-R-G-I-N at age twenty-six."

"My V-I-R-G-I-N-I-T-Y is none of your business."

"Sure it is," Dink said. "You were the first to know when I lost mine."

Jenna sent her a skeptical glance. "Not the first. I think Donny Keller knew before I did. And I didn't ask you to tell me. In fact I would rather you hadn't told me in such great detail."

Dink shrugged. "I felt it was my duty. Your mother certainly never made a push to clue you in."

"My mother told me all I needed to know."

Dink snorted loudly. "She told you no man would respect you once he'd had his tongue in your mouth."

"Dink!"

"Gross!" Jeff shouted at the same moment. "Yuk!"

"Gross, gross, yuk," Amelia repeated, giggling.

"If you two devil's spawn have finished your

oatmeal, go find Mrs. Hargreaves," Dink said, rolling her eyes.

"Give me a hug first . . . please," Jenna said, giving the children an apologetic smile.

"You're a terrible mother," she said to Dink as soon as the children left the room.

"No, I'm not. They think I'm cute. Now, let's get back to the subject at hand: The big *s*. Why didn't you ever do it with Greg?"

"Do it?" Jenna drew her head back, staring at her friend. "I can't believe you actually said 'do it.' How old are you, for heaven's sake?"

"Stop trying to change the subject. I want to know why you never slept with your fiancé."

"I meant to." Jenna frowned at the defensive note she heard in her own voice. "I just never got around to it."

"Are you listening to yourself? 'I meant to . . . I never got around to it.' Sweet Pete, Jenna, it sounds like you're making excuses for not taking out the trash. I wish you knew how wonderful it is. I wish you could see what happens to my mild-mannered Geoffrey when I get him in bed."

Jenna raised one slender brow. "Do you often have spectators?"

Dink giggled. "You know what I mean." She studied Jenna carefully. "Are you frigid?"

Jenna swallowed a groan. How could she have forgotten what Dink was like? A rat terrier had nothing on Dink once she got her teeth into a subject. From the day they first met, Dink had been Jenna's self-appointed psychoanalyst. At first she had spouted words of wisdom learned from her grandmother, folk truths about bottling up one's feelings. Later Dink had switched to more widely recognized experts like Freud and Jung for advice on how Jenna should feel and act, using words like *id* and *repressed urges* as she analyzed Jenna's dreams. Dink was determined to get her friend straightened out.

"No, Dink, I'm not frigid," Jenna said patiently. "I'm fastidious and cautious and maybe a little wary, but not frigid. Frigidity implies a strong, negative reaction to sex, and I've never had a strong reaction of any kind until—" She broke off and quickly took another sip of coffee. "I may not be a voluptuary like *some* people I know, but I'm definitely not frigid."

"Oh *ho*," Dink said, her eyes sparkling. "Back up there. What was that 'until—'? Until what? Until last night, when you stayed out all night with the Keeper of the Leprechauns?"

Jenna slowly raised her head to stare, narrow-eyed, at her friend. "Dink, darling, do you see the look in my eyes?"

Dink nodded slowly, warily.

"You've known me for most of my life," Jenna said, keeping her voice pleasant. "What does this look mean?"

"It means if I don't shut up, *this second,* you're going to stuff a dirty sock in my mouth."

"Exactly," Jenna said.

Without another word she pushed back her chair and walked out of the room.

In the hall Jenna heard voices coming from the sitting room and automatically switched her course. While she didn't relish negotiating the stairs again, there was a distinct possibility that she would smack the next person who commented on her Squeaky eyes, so she decided it would be more prudent to return to her room. Which she did and spent the next hour propped up in the outrageous acre of bed in her bedroom as she thumbed through a copy of the privately printed Aldham family history, a noticeably biased account of Geoffrey's ancestors. Although it wasn't the sort of thing she usually read, it had the advantage of being the only thing available.

In the back of the book there were several pages of diagrams, detailed layouts of each wing of the castle. Apparently Dink and Geoffrey were occupying only a tiny portion of the colossal keep; even if one discounted the gatehouse and outer buildings, there seemed to be miles and miles of unoccupied rooms in the main building. Dungeons and turrets. Weapons rooms and torture chambers. Treasure rooms and chapels.

As Jenna studied the sketches, it was brought home to her for the first time since her arrival that she was actually staying in an Irish castle, sleeping and eating and bathing in it. And if she wimped out, if she let those few anonymous rustles she had heard on the first day keep her from exploring it, she would never forgive herself.

Okay, she admitted silently, they were giggles, but they were very quiet giggles, and a spirit who giggled couldn't be all bad.

The decision made, Jenna set out, book in hand. Since she wasn't quite up to tackling a dungeon or torture chamber, she headed for the great hall to see where Geoffrey's progenitors had done their partying.

After taken several wrong turns and having to retrace her steps, Jenna finally entered the enormous, three-story-high hall.

At one end a fireplace big enough to house a family of four dominated the wall. Twelve massive iron chandeliers hung from wooden beams, and the walls were lined with freestanding torchères, each shoulder high and built to endure.

As she stood in the center of the cavernous room, Jenna could almost see the way it had been in the past. Long tables laden with food filled the room. And gathered around the tables were the hardy men who had come together after a raiding party.

The image brought a frown. Did the old Celts raid, or was that only the Vikings?

Jousting tournaments, maybe. Yes, that was better. After a hard day of jousting and doing chivalrous deeds the knights would have come to the hall to unwind and grab a little of the gusto, trying to one-up each other while throwing occasional insults and haunches of meat—untamed but generous were her knights—to the dogs and serfs huddling in the shadows.

At this point Jenna's fantasy ran into a slight hitch. She didn't know how to dress her phantom warriors. What did off-duty knights wear? Short, loose things? That would work, she decided with a grin. She hadn't seen *Camelot* in years, but short, sandwich-board jumpers with lots of muscled thigh showing sounded right.

At the head table would have sat the Top-notch Knight, the one who had saved more damsels and knocked the heads off more black knights than all the rest of the knights put together. The one with the cutest legs.

Jenna could see the scene more clearly now. Top-notch stood, one foot resting on a stool or varlet or something, as he raised a silver chalice of mead to the celebrating knights and swooning maidens in the crowd. After he had downed his drink in one long swallow, someone across the room—a pasty-faced, little guy who looked like the office suck-up—told a joke that made Top-notch throw back his head and laugh.

Jenna smiled as the contagious sound filled the corners of the enormous hall. All over the room heads turned to look at him, to share his amusement. Then Top-notch, in a movement that caught her off guard, turned his head toward Jenna.

In that moment all the laughter faded from the knight's brown eyes, and the look he gave Jenna took her breath away, as did his identity. Because her fictitious, partying paladin, the one with the gorgeous legs, was Keith.

At least she thought it was Keith. This was no gentle shepherd. It was the man she had only glimpsed in a shaft of moonlight the night before.

Now, in a vision created by shadows and imagination, he stood in full view. This man was a conqueror, a man who didn't stop until he got what he wanted, no matter the cost.

Jenna wanted to leave, but she couldn't make herself move. She didn't like this one bit. Things were happening inside her that she didn't understand, that she didn't want to understand.

In the count of a heartbeat the room had grown strangely airless. She couldn't catch her breath, and her pulse raced wildly as she felt herself being drawn into the fantasy that surrounded this dark knight.

She was not so much afraid of him as of the way he made her feel, because she knew if he took one step toward her, she would be lost. Lost in a dream that she would never find her way back from. If he—

"What're you doing, Aunt Jenna?"

Jenna must have jumped a foot, her heart trying to slam its way out of her chest, when the voice came from directly behind her. Whirling around, she saw Jeff standing in the doorway, staring up at her in bewilderment.

Wiping the perspiration from her face with a trembling hand, she drew in a deep breath. "Aren't you supposed to be having fingerpaint lessons or something?"

He made a contemptuous face. "That's baby stuff. I followed you. And you didn't even know I was there."

The last remnants of the fantasy shuddered through Jenna and finally let go. Bending her head, she considered her godson with a graceless frown. "So you want to learn something more useful, do you? I can help you with that. Let me explain the results of sneaking up behind a nervous person in a spooky old castle. Can you say 'myocardial infarction'? Come on, you little fiend, let's get out of here."

Minutes after they had left the great hall and its dark knight behind, an indignant Jeff was captured by the omniscient Mrs. Hargreaves, and Jenna was alone when she left the castle by a side door.

Exploring old castles was really not her thing, she told herself. Exercise was what she needed, vigorous exercise, something that would help keep her mind and body busy.

After interrogating one of the yardmen, Jenna

made her way to the garage. Inside, as promised, she found an array of traveling vehicles, vehicles from ages past, the sort usually found only in museums: an ornate carriage and a World War I–era touring car, among other things.

It was the World War II–era bicycle propped against a wall that Jenna had come to find. The bike was rudimentary compared with modern ones, but it had a sturdy look and would most likely survive a trip to the village and back.

Fifteen minutes later, as Jenna pedaled along the narrow, winding road, she planned her day. She would poke around the shops for a couple of hours, then she would buy food at the market and eat a leisurely lunch along the road on her way back to the castle.

It was a good plan, a fine plan, but unfortunately it went the way of most good plans. After parking the bike on the outskirts of the village, Jenna, flushed and noodle-kneed, walked down the main street—and spotted Carolyn Glendening-Waite.

The redhead stood on the opposite side of the street with her back to the small display window of an antique shop. Jenna stared in displeasure. Carolyn's thin lips tightened as she glanced at her wristwatch; she tapped her foot for a moment, then, after checking her watch again, turned her head to examine the pedestrians moving toward her from the north end of the street.

In a purely instinctive reaction Jenna swung around on her heels and began to move quickly in the opposite direction, slipping into the first alley she came to. If there was one thing she didn't need, it was another intimate chat with Miss Congeniality.

As it turned out, the near-disaster worked in Jenna's favor. Her cowardly exit carried her to a part of Slyne-Dun-Carrick she hadn't seen the day before. There were fewer big stores, more little shops with their wares spilling out onto the narrow street. And the people in this part of town were louder and busier.

At ease again, Jenna strolled slowly down the street, pausing when something caught her interest, surveying roughly crafted baskets and plump homemade bread with the same enthusiasm that she examined hand-knitted sweaters and exquisitely woven linen.

After she'd stopped to watch a young man with deft fingers assemble a straight-backed, wooden chair, Jenna looked up and saw Keith walking toward her.

She had become so involved in browsing that all thought of the night before had left her mind, and she found herself automatically raising a hand to hail him. And that was when the words she had spoken the night before came back to her. *Come with me.*

Cringing in embarrassment, Jenna turned and slipped quietly into the greengrocer's shop behind her.

Come with me.

The words tormented her. She would never be able to face him again without feeling that whispered plea between them.

"And so ends the magic," she said wryly as she watched Keith pass.

She waited ten minutes before making her way to the bicycle. Halfway back to the castle she realized one of the tires was gradually but determinedly going flat.

First Carolyn, then Keith, now a flat tire. Somebody was trying to tell her something.

Straddling the bike, Jenna planted her feet firmly on the ground and raised her face to the soft blue sky. "*Persecution* is an ugly word," she reminded the heavens.

Rest and relaxation. What a laugh. She would have been more relaxed in a war zone, she told herself as she wheeled the bicycle off the road. Leaving it propped against the rock wall that lined the road, she climbed over and made her way up a small, grassy knoll. As she sat with her arms around her knees, she spent a few minutes regretting the fact that she hadn't bought lunch as she had planned.

She should have stayed in town, she told herself. And if she had happened to run into Keith, she might have suffered a little embarrassment, but at least she wouldn't be sitting on the side of the road, staring at a bike with a flat tire as she listened to her stomach rumble.

On the up side, she hadn't thought about the Other Symptom once today, not even when she had been exploring the castle. That was something.

"Not food, but something," she muttered, then flopped back onto the soft grass, letting the sun and the Irish breeze ease her into relaxation.

Just for a while she would forget about her problems. She would forget she had made a fool of herself last night. She would forget about burnout, stress-related illnesses, and voices in her head. Just for a little while she would rest in the warm sunshine. Just for a while.

The sleep that claimed her only moments later was deep and dreamless.

Jenna felt herself coming awake and fought against it. She wanted to stay in the world of no cares for a while longer, but it was too late. Sleep was gone.

For a moment she lay with her eyes closed, feeling the sun on her face, then she raised her lids slowly. She wasn't sure how long she had slept, but the sun had definitely changed position since she last saw it.

Yawning, she stretched lazily, feeling oddly comfortable. But then, when she turned her head, she almost swallowed her tongue. Keith sat a foot away from her, his long legs bent, his chin resting on his knees as he gazed into the distance.

Twins, she decided, or triplets. Everywhere she looked there was a Keith.

"How long have you been here?" she asked, her voice still husky with sleep.

He shrugged. "An hour. Maybe more." He cut his eyes toward her. "I was watching you sleep."

She sat up. "Slow day? Not that I'm not willing to do my bit to keep the natives entertained, but watching a tourist snore and twitch and drool isn't my idea of a fun time."

"You didn't do any of those things. You sleep with the back of your hand against your cheek."

She felt heat flood her face. She would rather he had told her she snored. That wouldn't have seemed so intimate.

"What's bothering you?" he asked abruptly.

She glanced up, alarmed, then shook her head. "You have an uncomfortable habit of reading my mind, and I wish you would stop." She pushed hair from her forehead. "I made a fool of myself last night."

His lips twisted in a slight smile. "I was afraid you would see it that way."

She studied his face. "Which is why you didn't come in with me?"

Giving a rough laugh, he said, "The way I feel now, it seems an incredibly stupid thing for me to have done."

After a moment she glanced away from him. "I don't make a habit of propositioning men, you know," she said, her voice gruff with embarrassment. "In fact that was my very first time."

"Don't you think I know?" He sounded annoyed that she had felt compelled to explain. "Don't you know that I've seen what's at the heart of you, Jenna?"

Oh, criminy, she thought, growing even more uncomfortable. What on earth had she gotten herself into?

Watching her face, he muttered an incomprehensible expletive. "You're letting this get out of hand. Nothing happened last night that should cause you shame. So you can stop building those walls. Be warned, Jenna. I'll knock them down. Every damn one of them."

With a hand on her cheek, he turned her face toward him and smiled. "Stop looking for complications."

Giving her head a short shake, she said, "Wait a minute. Lord, it seems like I'm always saying that to you. But I don't know what's going on. I don't know—"

The rest of her protest was lost against his lips as he pressed her back to the grass. There was no wall between them now. Nothing except an explosion of emotion that made her forget every objection, every doubt. This was no simple physical union. This was a promise. It was a vow.

"That's better," he said, his voice rough as he raised his head slightly. "Now will you forget about your so-called proposition? I knew what you were trying to say. You were telling me that you didn't want a wonderful night to end. There's nothing in that to be ashamed of."

He was wrong of course. It had been her way of saying she wanted him to keep holding her. She had wanted it last night, and she wanted it now, in the daylight and stone-cold sober. But Jenna was grateful to him for an explanation that allowed her to save face.

She smiled up at him. "You're a nice man."

For an instant she saw the dark knight in his eyes, but then it was gone. It was the gentle shepherd who took her hand and helped her to her feet.

"Where are we going?" she asked as he urged her up the next rise.

"You don't think it was by way of an accident that you fell asleep just there, do you? The Little People took things in hand and gave your bicycle a puncture in the right place. This is my land, and Donegal House is just across the way here. And back that way"—he nodded toward the northeast—"is Aldham Castle. I'll walk you home."

She frowned. "I forgot about the bicycle.

Shouldn't we get it? I don't think it's something Dink particularly values, but it *is* part of Geoffrey's inheritance."

He smiled. "Don't worry yourself. I'll send one of the lads to fetch Sir Geoffrey's birthright."

As they walked across the meadow, Keith watched her from the corner of his eyes. He couldn't get a firm grasp on the workings of her mind. It was a mind much more intricate than he had at first thought. Intricate and injured and vulnerable. And even though she looked like an extremely lovely child, too young for cares, he sensed a world of pain in her past.

"I envy the people who knew you as a child," he said abruptly. "It would be a good memory to have."

"I don't think so," she said slowly, doubtfully. "I wasn't an attractive little girl. My parents wanted another son, but I think they would have made do with a daughter if she had been pretty, if she had looked like Mother—tall and elegant and blond. I take after my paternal grandmother, which means I had two strikes against me to begin with."

"Two?"

"I wasn't a duplicate of Mother, and I reminded my parents of a woman they would rather not remember. Grandmother Howard is something of an eccentric. Daddy ignores her, and Mother pretends she doesn't exist." Jenna frowned. "I haven't thought of Grandmother Howard in years. I should get to know her. If my parents don't approve of her, she's probably a terrific old lady. She might even like me . . . or not."

"Of course she'll like you. She'll love you. She couldn't do anything else."

She sent him a skeptical look. "If you say so."

"So you had a lonely childhood."

"Did I say that? I don't remember being lonely. Actually I don't think much about those days, back before I met Dink."

"When was that?"

"The first day of kindergarten, when I was five." She smiled wryly. "I was petrified, but I couldn't tell Mother. She wanted me to be brave, but I wasn't brave. Not at all. I was scared out of my mind. All the other children seemed so confident. And the teacher! The teacher looked like Hansel and Gretel's stepmother." She shrugged. "I wanted out, but I couldn't whine my way out, or Mother would hear about it. So I did the only thing I could think of."

"Which was?"

"I tried to escape . . . through the window." She gave a soft laugh. "It seemed like a good idea at the time. Everyone was horrified. Everyone, that is, except Dink. Dink laughed. She thought it was a wonderful joke and tried to get everyone in the room to come with me." Grinning, she added, "That was only the beginning. Dink and I were in trouble together for the rest of our career in the public school system."

He stared at the laughter sparkling in her violet eyes. So her friend Dink had kept her from freezing inside. He had never met Lady Georgiana, but already he liked her. "So you love your friend Dink."

She shrugged again. "I guess you could call it that. Sisterhood and all that jazz."

Jenna glanced at Keith from beneath her lashes. "Have you met Dink?"

"I haven't had the pleasure."

She stopped suddenly and placed her hand on his arm. "Come have lunch at the castle. I don't know about you, but I'm starved. I had intended to have lunch in the village, but—"

"The puncture put an end to that."

She opened her mouth to correct him, but swallowed the words instead. She didn't want him to know she had seen him in the village, that she had hidden behind a bunch of cabbage to avoid talking to him.

"Will you come?" she asked again. "I want you to meet Dink and her children."

He didn't answer immediately, and as the silence drew out, she shifted in discomfort. "Of course if you have other plans . . ." she began hesitantly.

"I don't," he said bluntly, then looked down at her and smiled. "But Lady Georgiana will have her hands fulls with her other guests. Besides, Donegal Farm is much closer. Have lunch with me. Mrs. Kennedy is back, so we'll get real food."

Her stomach rumbled loudly, answering for her.

It was early afternoon when Keith walked her the rest of the way to Aldham Castle.

"You mentioned your love for your friend Dink," he said, "but what about the other kind of love? Was there never a handsome football player in your life?"

"I had all the usual crushes in junior high and high school. I remember one in particular. Bobby Lee Masterson. I was too shy to let him know I liked him, so we became friends instead, and I had to listen to him agonizing over other girls. Then of course there was Greg."

"The ex-fiancé."

She nodded. "I can't believe I was ever that young. Back then I thought the universe revolved around his smile. For the entire time we were engaged, I found myself waking up in the middle of the night with my heart pounding, afraid I would do something wrong, afraid I would do something to disappoint him, terrified that I would do something that would make him stop loving me." She shook her head. "Sure enough, I did."

"And that's when you stopped believing?"

Jenna frowned. He was reading her mind again. Even Dink didn't know that Jenna didn't believe in love.

Shaking her head, she said, "No, that happened a long time before. And it wasn't just one thing. I started asking myself questions when I was a little girl. I found myself wondering how my parents really felt about me. The answer was obvious, even to a child." She paused. "Greg was an aberration. I was young and I wanted so badly to believe. I wanted someone to prove I was wrong. I wanted someone to show me that love—the giving, unselfish, forever-after kind of love—really existed. But it was just a fairy tale."

"A fairy tale," he murmured, then added, "I'm going to Limerick tomorrow to take care of some business. Will you go with me?"

She raised one brow. "In the pony cart?"

He laughed and shook his head. "In the Jaguar. A heathenish thing, but it gets me there."

"How . . . how quaint," she said, sputtering with laughter as, without hesitation, she agreed to go.

Six

"No. *No.* I said no! Just keep your hands off my things," Jenna ordered in exasperation.

For reasons of their own, Dink and the children had decided to visit Jenna in her bedroom while she dressed up for the trip to Limerick with Keith.

Swinging around on the stool, Jenna glanced at the two children, who sat politely on her bed. "Can't you control her? She's spilling powder all over the place."

Jeff merely rolled his eyes, but Amelia shrugged her tiny shoulders and sighed a little-girl sigh. "Mommy's a free spirit," she explained. "We can't do a thing with her."

"Oh yeah?" Jenna said as she removed a bottle of expensive perfume from the free spirit's hands. "A punch in the mouth always worked for me."

"Violence isn't allowed in our family," Dink said as she shifted her gaze to Amelia. "Orange sweater and red pants. Interesting. Innovative. You dressed all by yourself today, didn't you, punkin?"

Jeff considered his sister's clothes. "Maybe she's a free spirit too."

"*Free* and *tacky* are not synonymous." When the boy gave her a blank look, Dink added, "Take your sister to Mrs. Hargreaves and ask her to change the child's clothes."

As soon as the children were out of the room, Dink turned her attention to Jenna, speculation and curiosity shining in her green eyes.

"Stop looking at me," Jenna mumbled, leaning close to the mirror to apply mascara to her lashes.

"Are we a little edgy today?" Dink walked to stand behind her. "Let me see . . . what could be the reason? Cultural whiplash? Not enough roughage in your diet? Or maybe it's just plain old anticipation. Brought on by the fact that you're seeing a certain member of the local gentry for the *third day* in a row."

Refusing to rise to the bait, Jenna kept her features blank. After laying the mascara aside, she dusted the excess powder from her face with a sable brush, then stood, walked to the closet, and pulled out a lavender-and-cream sweater and matching cream wool skirt, all in silence.

But, as usual, not even a deliberate snub stopped Dink.

"You're going to Limerick with the shepherd," her blond friend mused, tapping her cheek with one finger. "You swore you would avoid the man like the plague, but you're going with him to Limerick. This is significant, Jeebo. This is *really* significant."

"Don't call me that," Jenna said through clenched teeth. "I told you never to call me that."

"Ha! Made you talk."

A laugh escaped Jenna before she could stop it. "Geoffrey's spoiled you. You think you're precious, even when you're being a pain in the butt. Why don't you leave and let me get dressed in peace?"

Dink moved her shoulders in a duplicate of her daughter's shrug and strolled casually toward the door. "Then I guess you don't want to know what I've learned about your mysterious man from the mist?"

Jenna jerked her head around. "Have you been asking questions about Keith? *Whom* have you been asking questions about Keith?"

"Calm down." Dink walked back to sit on the bed. "It was only Mrs. C., and she—"

"Mrs. Carradine? Your housekeeper? You talked to your housekeeper about my personal business?"

Dink stared at her for a moment. "You look like Jeff's gerbil did when Amelia squeezed it too hard. You need to watch that, Jenna. I'm telling you this as a friend, because frankly it's a little off-putting."

Jenna frustratedly exhaled a puff of air. "What did Mrs. Carradine say?"

"Before I tell you, may I make a small point here? A second ago you as good as called Keith your own personal business. . . . Okay, okay, don't get your drawers in a wad."

Settling against the bedpost, Dink shifted comfortably into her gossip mode. "You knew he lived here until he was twelve and then his mother took him to California? Well, according to Mrs. C. the divorce was a real mess. His mother's name was Juliet—that's not the messy part, I just thought it was ironic, considering the kind of woman she was. It seems she caused a big scandal by running wild."

"Running wild? What's that supposed to mean?"

"Pretty vague, huh? I figured Mrs. C. was exaggerating. You've seen the village. It stands to reason Slyne-Dun-Carrick's notion of running wild is wearing your skirt too short or something, but not in this case. Juliet started seeing a soul-searching writer, a would-be James Joyce, who was passing through the area, and apparently they got into some heavy stuff together. Of course Mrs. C. didn't give any details, but from the hints, I would say group sex and drugs at the very least. That sort of thing is frowned on even in swinging old London town, unless you're a rock star or a politician, so you can imagine the kind of uproar it caused around here."

Frowning, Jenna turned on the stool to face her friend. "If it really happened . . . I mean, if his mother was involved in that kind of thing, why didn't Keith's father get custody of him?"

"I asked the same question. According to Mrs. C., Sean Donegal was a peculiar man. Gentle, but proud and unbending. You know the kind. Soft voice, strong back, and even stronger principles. Keith was only twelve, but his father expected him to act and think like an adult. He gave him a choice. Stay at Donegal Farm and never see his mother again or go with her and never see his father again."

Gentle? Jenna thought in anger. The man was barbaric. How could he have forced such a decision on a child? Keith had told her that he had disappointed his father, but to Jenna's way of thinking, he had had no other choice.

Children feel such enormous responsibility. They tend to carry the weight of the world on their shoulders. A sensitive twelve-year-old would have gone with the parent who showed the greatest need. Keith had probably decided it was his job to take care of his mother.

"If you ever hear me whine about my rotten childhood again, I want you to slap my face," Jenna said, her voice tight with emotion.

Dink nodded. "It does make you stop and think, doesn't it? I tried to imagine my Jeff in the same situation, and I tell you, Jenna, it made me sick to my stomach."

"But Keith came back," Jenna said suddenly. "Or did he wait until after his father's death?"

"No, the old man died just last year." She paused. "Geoffrey and I didn't visit the castle more than a couple of times before Uncle Edward's death, but I think I remember seeing Sean Donegal in the village. He had one of those faces that looks like it was carved out of oak."

Dink shook her head. "No, it was Juliet's death that changed things. A little over five years ago she was killed in a boating accident. There were rumors at the time that she was drinking, but you know how rumors are. Anyway, immediately after the funeral Sean wrote to Keith and told him he could come home now."

"He phrased it like that?" Jenna asked, her voice incredulous.

"Yeah, I know." The blonde grimaced. "It struck me that way too. But Mrs. C. said Sean talked about it openly to his friends. He said now that 'the woman' was dead, he would let his son come home."

Jenna shivered. "That doesn't exactly sound repentant. I don't suppose there was a fatted calf prepared to welcome home the prodigal?"

"Are you kidding? The old man put Keith to work before his bags were unpacked. There were no arguments or anything like that. Gentle, remember? And on the surface things seemed fine between them, but Mrs. C. said sometimes Sean would shake his head and say that he was afraid living in America had killed the 'good Irish sense' in his son."

Dink stood and walked to the door. "Keith should have told him to take his farm and shove it. He should have told his father that he would come back when hell froze over."

"Maybe," Jenna murmured.

When the door closed behind Dink, Jenna swung around to face the mirror, but it wasn't her own image she saw there. She saw the face of a twelve-year-old boy, watching through the window of a car as everything he cared about grew smaller in the distance. Then she saw a young man, tormented and unable to sleep because his beloved Erin was calling to him.

The images were strong. Powerful enough and painful enough to still be with her later during the thirty-mile drive to Limerick.

Pretending to be absorbed by the passing scenery, she watched him from the corner of her eyes. Was it the past she saw in his face when the dark mood took over? Was the dark knight nothing more than the lingering pain of his childhood?

After the tenth time Jenna cut her eyes toward him, with the same expression on her beautiful face, Keith pulled the Jaguar to the side of the road and switched off the motor.

A moment passed before she glanced around and said, "Limerick has changed in the last couple of days. I'm almost sure I remember buildings, a river . . . people."

Leaning forward, he rested his arms on the top of the steering wheel and met her eyes. "You want to tell me what all the veiled looks are about? I feel like you're taking my temperature, long-distance."

"Veiled looks? Was I really—" She broke off, and bit her lip. "I've been listening to gossip," she admitted, an apology in her violet eyes.

He studied her face in an attempt to read her thoughts in her features. "Gossip," he murmured. "About the past or the present?"

"The past, I'm afraid."

Keith smiled in wry amusement. For him the past never went away, but it always surprised him to discover that other people were still interested in what was really ancient history.

"Tell me who told the story," he said, "and I'll let you know whether or not it's an accurate version."

"Mrs. Carradine."

"Nice lady," he murmured. "She's worked at the castle since she was a girl, you know. When I was a boy, I would visit her and Mrs. O'Doherty—she was the cook back then—in the kitchen, and the two of them would feed me little iced cakes and sweetened tea." He paused, remembering, then returned his gaze to Jenna. "I doubt Mrs. Carradine knows all the details, but I trust her not to have embroidered the truth to add spice to the story." He gave a short laugh. "Not that it needed any spice. What did she tell you?"

"Not me . . . Dink. I don't want you to think that I—"

He carelessly waved a hand. "Feel free to ask anyone you like. I wouldn't hold it against you." He smiled. "In fact it would please me to think you were interested enough to ask. Now, tell me what she said."

She shifted in her seat, as though the subject made her uncomfortable. "Not much really. She said when your mother and father divorced, you were forced to choose between them and . . . and then after your mother's death you were finally allowed to come home."

His laugh was more genuine now. "What was that, the *Reader's Digest* version? A little editing from you, and suddenly my life is rated G instead of Triple X. I think you're leaving some of it out to spare my feelings. Nice of you, but not necessary. I lived it. Hearing about it now doesn't hurt."

She made no comment, but her jaw tightened perceptibly. She was angry for him, he realized. He would have hated pity, but anger meant she took his troubles personally. Keith liked the idea. He liked it very much.

"What you heard about today is simply one side of the coin, Jenna," he said. Then after a moment's pause, he continued. "You were born and raised in Texas. I've been there a couple of times and I liked it. The people not only made me feel welcome, they did it with overwhelming all-encompassing exuberance."

She cut her eyes toward him. "Is that a nice way of saying Texans are loud?"

He laughed at her expression. "Do you mind?"

After a moment she shook her head. "No, I know

our faults. We're seen as ostentatious and outra-geous, self-aggrandizing and exclusionist. That's a cartoon Texan, but the thing about a caricature is that while it's an exaggeration, it's an exagger-ation based on truth. The rough edges are part of what I love about Texas. Put the good and bad together and you have something truly extraordi-nary. But what does that—"

She met his eyes and broke off. "I see," she said quietly. "You're saying that I can't define your parents or your childhood by a single event."

Smiling, he nodded. "We Irish are a complex people, so don't ever take what you see on the surface for the total. This small island is the most wonderful place on earth. The land and the people who work it can be harsh, but we take pride even in the harshness. It's just another part of what makes it unique."

He straightened away from the steering wheel and reached down to start the engine. "Two sets of parents, yours and mine, all intelligent, educated people. But I don't think any one of the four spent a lot of time studying child psychology. There's nothing either of us can do about that now. It would be a mistake to forget the past, but it would be a bigger mistake to let it dictate the terms of your future. And do you know what the biggest mistake of all would be?" he asked as he pulled back onto the road.

"What?"

"Wasting our time together with a lot of intense, meaningful dialogue. This day was made espe-cially for nonsensical talk and hour upon hour of mind-boggling jocularity."

"What a silly word," Jenna said with a spurt of

laughter. "You wouldn't get away with using a word like that in Dallas."

Keith was right, Jenna decided as they continued on their way to Limerick. The past was a bottomless pit, and if you weren't careful, it would swallow up everything in sight, every thought, every feeling. She wasn't going to let that happen. Not today.

Having made the decision, she felt suddenly lighter. She didn't know why she felt so relieved, but that was another thing she wasn't going to examine at the moment. Jocularity was the order of the day.

Keith's business in Limerick took little more than half an hour, and then he was free to show her the sights. Although he played tour guide with dedicated fervor, because they were both determined to be silly, Jenna didn't believe even half of his outrageous tales.

They were in English Town, an island completely encircled by the Shannon, when Jenna finally questioned his narrative.

"That's about the thousandth place where Saint Patrick slept. The man got around more than George Washington. It's not that I doubt your word, you understand, but why would he spend the night at a tobacco shop?"

Before he could answer, she glanced at a man who stared at her from the shadowy doorway of the store. "Saint Patrick may have slept here," she muttered, "but this obviously isn't where he cast out all the snakes."

Chuckling, Keith took her arm, and they moved

on past the shop. "That was in County Mayo," he said, "up on Croagh Patrick. Maybe you'd like to go there. Thousands do every year, walking the whole way in their bare feet. The path goes straight up, to the saddle below the peak's north face. Below, you can see the Murrisk Peninsula jutting out into Clew Bay. You go through the saddle and climb up the summit from the back. The final ascent is a steep scree of loose, jagged rocks that slide under your feet with every step. It's always raining up there, but people still go, just so they can stand in the spot where the saint stood as he drove the snakes over the precipice into the sea."

She stopped walking and looked around. It had rained earlier, and the damp streets glistened in the hide-and-seek sunlight. "Standing here, listening to you," she said softly, "I can see why they do it. Climb the mountain, I mean. In the United States we rush hysterically toward the future and never bother looking over our shoulders to see our country's past. We read about it, but we no longer feel it. Ireland's different. The past is right here, isn't it? In the air and everywhere you look. It would be no great shock to turn a corner and find Turlough O'Connor or Brendan of Clonfert walking down the street toward you."

"How do you know about Turlough O'Connor and Brendan of Clonfert?"

"I read a book on the flight over. Irish history, made quick and easy for short-attention-span Americans. You've had an awful lot of history, and most of it was confusing, so don't ask me what Turlough or Brendan did to get in a history book. I simply happen to like the names of your kings."

"Tourist," he said scornfully.

They laughed a lot during their day together, and there were times when he would grab her hand and take off running. She didn't ask what they were running to or from. She simply ran with him. It was that kind of day.

And like all days, it eventually had to end. It was late afternoon when they left Limerick behind and headed for home, stopping at a noisy, crowded country inn for dinner.

Although the other diners weren't friends and neighbors of Keith's, like the people she had met at the fair of Slyne-Dun-Carrick, they included the newcomers in their conversations just the same, insisting that she and Keith choose sides in heated, incomprehensible arguments.

Jenna loved it, but when she imprudently joined a debate over whether a national language influenced a country's politics, taking first one side, then the other to keep the argument going, Keith took her arm and pulled her through a side door.

"You fiend," he said, his dark eyes gleaming with laughter as he gazed down at her. "In a couple of minutes they're going to start throwing chairs and potted plants at each other."

"It's one way to win a debate," she said, still exhilarated by the argument. "Whoever is left standing at the end is the most eloquent."

At that moment, in the west, the sun broke through the clouds just in time to set. In that one last burst of glorious light the garden was filled with splashes of orange, pink, and red, the hues blindingly beautiful, spectacularly wild. Then, the brief moment of glory gone, the colors gentled and settled back into their original roles: to give solace to the eye and heart.

Here was peace, Jenna thought as she breathed deeply of the serenity. Not a world full of peace, just one small corner.

There had been times in her life when Jenna was happy. There were times when she considered herself reasonably contented, but even during the happiest, most contented times, when she looked deep enough, she always found a restlessness in her soul. Tonight it was gone. Tonight as she looked inward, she found peace. She didn't know if the change was permanent or merely a temporary aberration. At the moment she didn't care. It was that kind of night.

"Who was that man we saw in the park?" she asked as they walked along a small pathway through the garden. "He was small and outraged. A Muppet with an attitude. I couldn't understand what he was saying, but the crowd was really getting into it."

"That was old Hugh. He was urging the crowd to rise up and rebel and make Limerick a separate kingdom again . . . with him as its king. I'm afraid he tends to confuse parts of his life with Brian Boru's, but he does no harm. Limerick wouldn't be the same without old Hugh."

She cast a glance at him. "You're a nice man. A tolerant man. I wish I were more like that. When I see people like him, I want to shake them and say, 'You want to stand around all day talking? Then talk about something useful. Tell them what's happening in the rain forests and in the oceans. Get a real cause, for Pete's sake.'"

He gave a soft laugh. "Americans are more

involved with the world. To an Irishman, Ireland *is* the world. We rarely look beyond our borders because the things that are truly important to us are happening right here. You won't find a man, woman, or child here who doesn't feel passionate about this small green island. Passionate and possessive."

He had stopped walking moments before. Now, with a hand on her throat, he raised her head and fixed his dark gaze on her lips. "Those feelings run deep, alanna." The words were a husky whisper. "Ireland is our own, and we're miserly with what belongs to us."

As she met his eyes in the dusky light, her breath caught in an inaudible gasp. This was no gentle shepherd, no dark knight, no laughing tour guide. All the sensuality in the world came together in his dark eyes. He was not asking, not begging, he was *demanding* that she step across an invisible line and join him.

Shock shivered through her, and she started to shake her head in denial, but he was already lowering his head, already touching his mouth to hers. Instantly she knew this was no kiss of comfort, no kiss of simple pleasure, as were the kisses they had shared before.

She would pull away in a minute, she told herself. She would step back and find the gentle shepherd or the dark knight. In a minute.

But she waited too long. Heat traveled from their joined lips and began to spread through her body, gathering strength and momentum as it went, and then his mouth moved on hers and a flash of heat settled in her middle.

She felt lit from the inside, a glow in the center

of erotic sensation. She wanted to run from the feeling even as she tried to move closer to it physically.

A harsh sound came from him, and he moved with her in his arms, beyond the path, beyond the row of flowers to the shadows of a tree. He pressed her back against the smooth trunk and settled his body against hers in an urgent thrust. And suddenly Jenna forgot all about running. She would have fought anyone who tried to take this feeling away from her. Because, now at last, she *knew* this man. These were the arms she had longed for those nights so long ago; it was this emphatic embrace she had craved.

There was wildness in them both. Keith didn't know where it began, in her or in him. He only knew that in the space of a few minutes everything had changed. The night, the woman in his arms, his whole life.

He moved his lips to her ear, to her warm, smooth throat, and felt her pressing into him, as though, like him, she couldn't get close enough. He felt like an alcoholic faced with the knowledge that this taste of wine was the last drop in the bottle. In the same way, the savoring of her, the reveling in the taste and feel and scent of her, was a pleasure tinted with desperation.

When her hands came to his neck to pull his mouth to her breast, a groan came from deep in his chest. Nothing—in their time together, in what had thus far transpired in his life—had prepared him for what he was feeling now. Some primitive instinct seemed to be at work here. The veneer laid on by civilization was being stripped away from them both, leaving emotions that were as old as time and absolutely honest. He wanted to tell her. He wanted to share what he was feeling and make certain it was the same for her.

A moment later she pulled his head up, searching for his lips with her own, and then, in what felt like a body blow, her words reached him.

"Enchanted Irish dreams," Jenna whispered huskily against his lips. "And I didn't even know I was dreaming them."

Suddenly Keith's fingers were digging into her shoulders and he was holding her away from him. "Not a dream," he said, his voice hoarse with something very close to anger. "I'm real, Jenna. Look at me."

She blinked, once, twice, trying to bring him into focus through the misty remnants of passion.

He shook her. "I said look at *me*. Wipe out this garden. In your mind transport the two of us back to Dallas. Instead of roses and moonlight, there are traffic lights and glass towers around us." He paused to let her see the new vision. "Now look at me."

Shock traveled through her. If this were Dallas, she wouldn't be in his arms. Because Keith was the kind of man who made her feel too much. He was the kind of man who could hurt her.

He was the kind of man who could walk away with her heart.

That wasn't what Jenna wanted. That wasn't what she wanted at all.

"It's your fault," she said in a tight whisper. "You started this with your, 'So you've finally come' talk. Leprechauns and Queen Brianna . . . the Little People who got into my head and brought me here. You have no right to turn around and—"

"You're right." He drew in a deep, harsh breath. "Okay, dammit, I admit it. You're right."

Taking her arm, he led her to a wooden bench and sat down with her. "I can't explain," he said after a moment. "Mostly because I'm as confused as you are. When I said that about you finally getting here, it was a joke. At least I thought it was at the time. You reminded me of someone."

Jenna frowned, disliking the idea. She wasn't a copy of someone. She was herself.

"Something is happening between us, Jenna," he said with quiet intensity. "I know you feel it too. It's too . . . too big to be one-sided. I simply want— I think we should explore it without fantasies, yours or mine, getting in the way."

Cold fear rushed through her with speed. What happened to nonsensical talk and mind-boggling jocularity? Where had they lost the wonderful silliness?

And then anger took hold, dissolving the fear. With a few words Keith had forced Jenna to see what she had been doing. She prided herself on being realistic. But now she understood that reality was a part of where she lived. She had left it behind in her apartment along with her blue flannel robe and her scuffed running shoes.

She was vacationing in a dreamland, and that was the way she wanted to keep it. With no conscious plan, she had intended her feelings for Keith to take the place of vacation snapshots. Someday in the future she would take the memories out, look at them, and smile with distant, remembered pleasure.

That was why she had been uneasy with the pain hearing of his childhood had brought, she told herself now. It made him too real. And that was why the relief had been so overwhelming when she agreed to put aside all serious thoughts for the day. Anger, pain, and regret were not the pictures she wanted in her vacation album.

And apparently Keith knew that. He knew more about how her mind worked than she did. Jenna resented that. She resented the hell out of it. And most of all, she resented him for ruining her snapshot-memory of this day.

"I think I'd like to go home now," she said stiffly.

He gave a rough laugh. "I figured you would react this way."

"Stop doing that! You don't know me. You don't know what's inside me. You're just making a lot of wild guesses."

"I know you're pushing me away because I'm getting too close. And I know you're mad as hell at me for shaking you up."

"I'm pushing you away because we've known each other three days," she lied, her voice rigid now. "I thought we had a nice friendship going, then you start trying to—" She broke off and drew in a shaky breath, then rose to her feet. "Just take me home."

On the drive back to the castle neither of them spoke. That suited Jenna just fine. She felt bruised and drained, and she didn't want to talk to him again. She didn't want to see him again.

When they pulled into the courtyard, he switched off the engine, got out, and walked around to the passenger side. But Jenna already had the door open and was stepping out. She didn't need his help. For anything.

He stood looking down at her for a long, silent moment. "I wasn't trying to get a commitment from you, you know," he said quietly. "I simply wanted you to consider the possibility that there is some substance to this thing between us."

"You ask too much." She avoided his eyes as she walked past him toward the front door.

She had reached the entrance and her hand was on the latch when she heard him say, "Maybe we were meant to be nothing more than friends, but if you run, Jenna, we'll never find out."

She didn't answer. She didn't even look back as she opened the door and walked inside.

Seven

There were times during the next two days when Jenna couldn't remember exactly why she was so angry with Keith, but that didn't keep her from avoiding him. She took no more walks through the countryside, and if she went to the village, she went with a group. She mixed and mingled with the other houseguests. She dazzled them with her sparkling wit. She smiled until her teeth hurt.

Now that Geoffrey had finally arrived from London, Dink was happy. Not only did she have daily access to the man who spoiled her outrageously but the numbers at dinner were even now. Jenna was most often paired with Ralph—she went out of her way to make sure she was paired with Ralph—but occasionally Max managed to catch her alone, and more than once Jenna found herself ducking into a closet or a dusty alcove to avoid a man who seemed intent on either seducing a casual acquaintance or annoying his wife.

Although the former would take place when hell

froze over, in the latter Max was successful. Carolyn was most definitely annoyed. In the space of a few days the redhead had gone from treating Jenna with patrician disdain to open nastiness. She used each of Dink's carefully planned outings and entertainments as a forum for her own private war, a war that escalated with each encounter.

"We could take a break, dear," Carolyn called from across the tennis net. "You're looking flushed."

Jenna and Ralph had set out an hour earlier to play a lazy game of singles, but somehow it had turned into a foursome, and a battle was being fought between the Redcoats and the backward colonists.

"It's always been a puzzle to me why Americans perspire so much more extravagantly than the British," Carolyn said in a careless aside as she prepared to serve.

"Maybe because Brits are so uptight, they can't even let go of a little sweat," Jenna muttered.

Ralph, overhearing the remark, let out a loud yelp of laughter.

"What was that, Jenna?" the redhead called. "What did you say?"

"I don't think you want to know, darling," Max told his wife with a grin. "We'll just say the opposition returned that volley admirably."

Unfortunately Jenna was better at returning words than tennis balls. She and Ralph were no match for the Glendening-Waites. The couple played with precision and deadly determination. They played as though it mattered.

After the game, as Jenna walked off the grass

court, Carolyn caught up with her. "You're out of your league, you know," the redhead said.

"You won't get an argument on that," Jenna said, her voice slightly breathless from exertion. "Tennis isn't my game."

"What is?"

Jenna stopped and exhaled in a resigned sigh. "I beg your pardon?"

"What are you up to, Miss Howard? Georgiana told us you came here to take a break, a *petit sursis* from your kitchen towels or whatever it is you design, but I've been watching you. You seem to have the mistaken idea that you belong here. Yesterday, in the village, the way those Flaherty children called you Aunt Jenna, if it weren't *so damnably pathetic*, it would have been laughable."

The venom in the woman's voice was so intense, Jenna openly stared in reaction. "All right, let's do it," she said, pulling the sweatband from her head as she turned to face Carolyn squarely. "Let's get this out in the open and over with. I'm no good at beating around the bush, so I'll be blunt. I have no interest in your husband. Not now, not ever. I don't like him. No, let me make that clearer. Your husband has slimy manners, sneaky eyes, and no morals . . . and I'm leaving out his worst qualities. If I could get a *petit sursis* from his stalking, it would be heaven. So you can cancel any plans you might have to cut my throat."

Carolyn glared for a moment, then she threw back her head and laughed. It was an unpleasant, grating sound that had a somewhat hysterical quality to it.

"Max?" she said, her voice high, the words sharp. "You think this is about Max?"

And then, before Jenna could respond, Carolyn turned and walked away.

Jenna was scratching the top of her head with her tennis racket when Ralph joined her. Shooting an inquisitive glance at him, she said, "You're not by any chance having an affair with Carolyn, are you?"

He choked. "Wha— You— *Carolyn?* Good grief, no. I'm not that brave. If her ancestors weren't Druids, I'll pay for lying. Why would you ask something like that?"

"I'm trying to figure out why I'm number one on her hit list. Not Max. Not you." She shrugged. "Why?"

"Definitely not me," he said with a shudder as he ran a hand through his curly blond hair. "I wouldn't worry about it if I were you. She's the sort who would turn antagonistic toward any woman who outshines her."

Jenna smiled. "You're sweet. And thanks for not saying the reason I outshine her is all my extravagant American perspiration."

With a chuckle he threw an arm around her waist, and together they walked back to the castle.

Jenna liked being with Ralph. He was the kind of man she had dated in the past, the kind of average American male she would have met had she gone to Bora Bora for her vacation. She could relax with Ralph. She could talk business with him. And when he flirted, she had no reservations about flirting back. It was the kind of thing one did on a vacation. It was the kind of thing one did while running frantically from one's true feelings.

Late that same evening Jenna sat at the window of her bedroom, leaning against the slightly damp embrasure as she looked out at the night. It had been an extremely active day, and she should have been exhausted, but the old familiar restlessness was in her blood tonight, keeping sleep away.

In the courtyard below, a heavy mist softened the edges of the stone walls, making the landscape look strangely pliable.

What was that nursery rhyme? she wondered. *One misty, moisty morning.* It wasn't morning, but the misty and moisty part fit.

As she idly surveyed the cushiony terrain, her gaze passed over a rounded shape, then seconds later traveled back to it. In the same way a child finds dragons in the clouds, Jenna found a man-shape in the shrouded landscape. A smoky, soft-edged man, squatting on his heels in the mist.

Studying the figure, she tried to picture the courtyard as it appeared in daylight. What was near the well that, with the addition of fog, took on the shape of a man? Not a stick-figure man, but a fully developed man who rested on his haunches, his head tilted back as he gazed up at her window.

In the next moment Jenna's breath caught in her throat and her heart began to pound. The shape was moving, growing larger, as though the vapor-phantom were rising to his feet.

And then, with a whirling of mist, the man-shape was gone.

Swinging away from the window, Jenna held a trembling hand to her wildly racing heart. She stumbled across the room and climbed into bed, squeezing her eyes shut as she made a futile effort to squeeze her mind shut as well.

Jenna ran down the stairs, moved briskly across the hall, and walked into the breakfast room. After filling a cup with coffee and grabbing a muffin, she joined Dink and the children at the table.

"Where is everyone?" she asked.

"Geoffrey and the other men went out early to shoot at helpless creatures," Dink said, her voice listless. "Anne is harassing the gardener, and dear, delightful Carolyn is still in bed."

"Good, I wanted to—"

"I love you, Aunt Jenna," Amelia said, her cupid's-bow lips covered with strawberry jam.

"I love you, too, doodlebug. Dink, I need to—"

"I love her more than you." Jeff belligerently put both elbows on the table. "I'm bigger than you and I love her harder."

"You're bigger, but you're stupider." Amelia gave her brother a close-up view of her food-coated tongue, then turned to Jenna. "Are we going to talk about your V-G-R-T today, Aunt Jenna?"

"No, we're not," she said firmly. "And we're not going to compare me with Jeff's gerbil or Squeaky or any other animal you've owned in your young lives. I have something to discuss with your mother."

Dink, who in the last couple of days had been bothered by morning sickness, glanced up from an awesome contemplation of her breakfast plate.

"Have you ever noticed how truly ugly an egg is?" she asked with a shudder. "It's like a big, bulging eye, taunting me, daring me to eat it without being sick."

"You can't be sick right now," Jenna said, her tone implacable. "I need to talk to you."

Dink carefully covered her plate with her napkin, making sure that no scrap of food was visible. "So talk."

"Your guests will be leaving next week."

"I've heard that rumor." Dink warily pushed her plate away, as though she were afraid that, at any moment, the food might try to leap up at her. "I'll believe it when I see it."

"Dink, you're not paying attention! Everyone's leaving. Don't you think you should, you know, do something for them before they go?"

"I've taken them fishing and to boxing matches and to hurling competitions . . . without ever once mentioning that *hurling* is a revolting word and in no way related to football. I've pretended I can tell the difference between Cecil and Anne, and that I like Carolyn and Max. I've fed the whole bunch for five days. What else am I supposed to do for them?"

Jenna stirred her coffee for a moment, then glanced up. "Oh, I don't know," she murmured, keeping her voice casual, "maybe a formal party?"

When Dink stopped choking, Jenna said, "You know how much you like hauling out those seriously baroque Aldham 'jools.'" She leaned forward eagerly. "Here's an idea: We could do a torchlight tour of the more grisly rooms in the castle. Come on, Dink, it'll be fun," she coaxed. "And since I'm here to do all the work, it won't be too much of a strain on you. It's a terrific way of killing two birds with one stone."

"What birds? What stones?"

"Invite the people in the area as well. It's about time you got to know your neighbors. The squires, or whatever you call the leading citizens around here, are beginning to look crosswise at the 'queer folk up t' the castle.'"

"You're up to something," Dink said, her eyes narrowed in suspicion. "When you get this chummy, I always know you're up to something."

Jenna made a careless sound of denial. "I'm trying to help you, for heaven's sake. This is Geoffrey's ancestral home. You should make a push to become involved with the people in the area. Castles don't come free, you know. You didn't just inherit a hulking monstrosity and some slow-witted ghosts. You inherited obligations."

Dink studied her face. "Missing the man from the mist, are we?"

Drawing back, Jenna inhaled a sharp breath. "I hate you, Dink."

"Well, aren't you?"

"Like crazy," she admitted, slumping in her chair. "I stayed awake all night trying to get him out of my head. How did you know?"

"When have you ever been able to hide anything from me? Didn't I know the exact day—the day after your fourteenth birthday—when that fat kid with the braces kissed you? Didn't I know when you found out about your art scholarship? Didn't I know when—"

Jenna snorted. "Tee Boy Ledbetter was stocky, not fat, and you knew about all those things because I told you."

"I would have known anyway." She rose to her feet. "Okay, so what are we going to do about this party?"

Eight

The Aldham jewels were sent for, and invitations to Dink's gala, handwritten by Jenna, went out by special messenger. The short notice probably caused a few raised eyebrows, but around Dink raised eyebrows were a permanent condition, so Jenna figured the good citizens of Slyne-Dun-Carrick might as well get used to it.

Only hours after the invitations went out, acceptances began coming in, and every time the telephone rang, every time she heard the sound of the front-door knocker reverberating through the hall, Jenna held her breath, wondering if this time it would be Keith.

She was beginning to think she had planned the whole affair for nothing when, three days before the party, one of Keith's men dropped around with a note accepting the invitation.

The instant Jenna knew he would be there, her adrenaline kicked into overdrive, and she threw herself into the last-minute preparations with dedicated zeal.

The caterers were under Mrs. Carradine's jurisdiction, but the rest fell on Jenna's shoulders. It was she who made the decision to use a local band rather than a string quartet from Limerick; she who made sure the rooms included in the torchlight tour were free of any unwelcome inhabitants, deceased or otherwise; she who was in charge of turning the dusty great hall into a reasonable facsimile of a ballroom. It was Jenna who was so busy, she had no time to worry.

But then the night of the gala arrived, and she found time. She sat at the dressing table in her bedroom, applying her makeup, and suddenly stopped to study her reflection in the mirror, wondering for the first time exactly what she was trying to accomplish tonight.

If it was so important that she be with Keith, why hadn't she gone to Donegal Farm? Why hadn't she simply gone for a walk? Sooner or later he would have turned up.

Laying the eyeshadow brush carefully aside, she leaned closer to the mirror, searching her frowning eyes for the truth.

And then she knew. She was doing exactly what Keith had asked her to do. She was making an effort to see him. Really see him.

A big part of Jenna's life in Dallas was given over to socializing: cocktail parties, business banquets, charity balls. The party was as close as Jenna could get to placing Keith in the real world.

Who would she see when he walked in tonight? she wondered. The man who had become a star player in her wild Irish dreams? Or an ordinary man who wouldn't bring a second look from her if she passed him on the streets of her hometown?

Groaning, she pushed a hand through her hair and leaned her elbows on the dressing table. She didn't know what she would see, and she didn't know how she would react to what she would see. She didn't even know what she was hoping to see. The only thing certain was that tonight would bring answers.

After tonight she would be able to move on, she told herself moments later as she pulled her hair to the top of her head, then with a grimace let it fall back to her shoulders. Next she tried a twist at the nape of her neck, but with a sound of irritation she released it and began searching through the clutter on the tabletop for the mother-of-pearl combs she knew were there somewhere. Maybe if she swept it back just a little on the sides—

"Leave it down."

Jenna jumped and swung around on the stool. "Whatever happened to that quaint old custom of knocking?" she asked her friend and hostess.

"Leave your hair loose," Dink repeated as she, with carefully slow movements, lowered her swollen body to sit on the bed. "If I had tons of naturally curly hair, I wouldn't keep it scraped back like you do. I'd flaunt the stuff. Besides there's a little bit of wildness in your eyes tonight. Might as well make it a theme."

"Speaking of wild," Jenna said, running her gaze over Dink's electric-blue caftan and the chandelier hanging around her neck. "It beats me how you can make that grotesque thing look regal, but you do. You're gorgeous tonight, Dink."

Her friend responded with a loud snort. "Sure, if

you like prehistoric fertility goddesses. What are you going to wear?"

Rising to her feet, Jenna went to the closet and pulled out a satin dress. White and free of adornment, it had the look of a floor-length slip.

Dink let out a low whistle between her teeth. "You're out to do damage to somebody. You don't wear a thing like that, you spray it in the air and walk through it." She cut her eyes to Jenna. "It'll look sensational with your black hair, but are you sure you know what you're doing? Anything you wear under it is going to show."

Jenna walked to the bureau and opened the top drawer. "Not this," she said, holding up a tiny scrap of white silk. "What about you? You're probably into industrial-strength underwear by now."

Dink's response was to throw a pillow at Jenna's head. "Stay away from Geoffrey tonight, or I'll make sure you're short-sheeted for the rest of your visit."

"Stupid," Jenna said, laughing. "Geoffrey thinks it's Christmas every time you walk into the room."

"You're right of course." The blonde grabbed the bedpost and hoisted herself upright. "But just in case, I think I'll go find my man and plant a few indecent ideas in his head so the only thing he'll be thinking of tonight is bedtime and me."

Jenna watched the door close behind Dink, then began to dress, uncertainty creeping up on her once more.

She wasn't present when the first guests arrived. She was in the kitchen instead, pretending that her help was needed there. But when Mrs. Carradine finally shooed her out, she fell in step with a group on their way to the hall at the back of the castle.

Bypassing Dink and Geoffrey, who stood at the wide entrance to greet their guests, Jenna looked out across the spacious room.

At some point in the past the wrought-iron chandeliers had been wired for electricity, but the illumination they offered was meager, so additional lighting, concealed by plants and silk screens, had been added to strategic spots around the room.

Still, the room wasn't as bright as a modern ballroom, and the overall effect was that of a cavern. Not bad, she decided. Not bad at all.

In front of the fireplace, on a hastily built and carefully camouflaged platform, the five-piece band played an old Irish lullaby, and the delicate sound filled the room, drifting in and out of clusters of festively dressed people.

Cecil and Anne Coombs, both dressed in black, were dancing and, as always, looked as though they were having a wonderful time. Max and Carolyn stood next to each other near an outer door but, as always, were carefully ignoring each other. The former laughed down at a blushing young woman while the latter, looking beautifully untouchable in an emerald-green gown, examined the room with contemptuous amusement.

Although she hadn't expected to, Jenna recognized quite a few people from her day at the fair. Ralph was dancing with the woman who had given Jenna a recipe for plum cake. Michael and Sara Flaherty stood in a group of their relatives, brothers and sisters, parents and grandparents. Thomas, Jamie, and Paddy danced with a trio of wives. Mr. O'Brien, the rotund man who had moved like a Ping-Pong ball caught in a windstorm at the street dance, was hovering near the food tables. Fiona Blair was walking around the room on the arm of a man with rust-colored hair and an air of pleasant confusion.

But the person Jenna needed to see, the man she most wanted to see, was nowhere in sight. Half an hour later when Dink and Geoffrey left the door and began to mingle, he still wasn't there.

His note said he would be pleased to come, she reminded herself. It said he looked forward to the gathering.

"He's obviously champing at the bit," she muttered, turning her gaze away from the entrance. "Probably broke a leg in his rush to get here."

Pinning a smile on her face, Jenna began to give her attention to those of Dink's guests who actually showed up. She danced with Ralph. She danced with Cecil and Max and Geoffrey. She danced with the rotund man, who turned out to be the father of either Thomas, Jamie, or Paddy.

An hour later, as she stood between Michael Flaherty's father and his father-in-law, making a halfhearted effort to avert a political discussion, Jenna's gaze turned once more toward the entrance to the ballroom.

Her heart raced, her breath caught in her throat, and everything in the room faded. The music, the lights, the people—all disappeared. There was only one man. One man with dark hair and dark eyes, dressed in dark evening clothes, who stood staring at her across the room.

Shoving her glass into Mr. Flaherty's hand, Jenna began to move toward him, but before she had taken two steps, others in the room spotted him and began to hail him. Moments later he was surrounded by people.

"That's Keith?"

Jenna cut her eyes to the woman whose presence she had been unaware of until that moment and nodded.

"And you've been avoiding him?" Dink asked, her eyes wide. "That's crazy, Jeebo. Just plain crazy."

"Don't call me that," Jenna murmured without conviction, her voice distracted, her attention still focused on the man across the room.

She had wondered if he would appear ordinary to her tonight, Jenna reminded herself with a wry smile. Dink was right, she was crazy.

In the next few minutes Jenna saw Keith move toward her over and over again, but each time he was stopped by an acquaintance. It was only when she and Dink began to organize the crowd for the torchlight tour that he managed to reach her side for a moment.

"I'm sorry I was late," he said, speaking quickly, as though he were afraid they would be interrupted. "I had to take Duffy to the doctor. No, he's all right. One of the horses kicked him in the leg, but nothing was broken." He dropped his voice, his gaze drifting over her body. "That dress . . . my God, alanna, that dress." And then, just as he had feared, people came between them, and Jenna was swept away by Ralph and Mr. O'Brien.

The tour was as successful as Jenna had hoped. At least it was a big hit with the guests. For herself Jenna only wanted it to be over so she could finally catch a moment with Keith. When they reached the dungeon, the last stop on the midnight excursion, Geoffrey gave an exaggerated, tongue-in-cheek account of the room's past occupants. Afterward Jenna watched the others leave, laughing and squealing when they brushed against something or someone in the flickering light.

She watched, but she didn't join them. She was going to stay where she was. Keith would find her. He always found her, and maybe here in the dungeon they could have a few minutes alone. There were things she needed to tell him. She needed to ask him about the misty, moisty man in the courtyard. She needed to tell him that she had finally "seen" him.

Time passed, and since she couldn't see her watch, it seemed to pass very slowly. Just as she was deciding that Keith had been waylaid by one of his friends, she heard the voices. Whispering. Urgent sounds muted by vast quantities of rock and space.

For a brief moment Jenna thought the Other Symptom had chosen this night to reappear, but then she realized the whispering wasn't coming from inside her head. It was coming from the hall outside the dungeon.

Cautiously feeling her way through the darkness, Jenna left the dungeon and moved toward the sound. And then, in a circle of light from a freestanding torchère, she saw them. A man and a woman.

Keith had stayed behind after all. But instead of finding Jenna, he had found Carolyn. They stood close together next to the wall, her hand on his arm. And as the redhead stared up at him, there was an expression on her face that Jenna had never seen before. Carolyn looked pleasant. She looked vibrant and alive. She looked damned seductive.

Something foreign and uncomfortable began to swell inside Jenna's chest, then a moment later she was pressed against the wall, unable to catch her breath, her head swimming, her eyes closed.

As Jenna had watched them together, feeling the explosion of anger and pain, she had finally seen the truth inside her. Now, at last, she *knew*.

Using the darkness to hide her movements, Jenna slipped past them. When she was well out of hearing range, she held up her skirt and ran, in and out of dark corridors, letting instinct guide her. She didn't slow down until she had reached the terrace outside the great hall.

A row of windows left puddles of light on the uneven stones, but Jenna avoided them and walked farther into the shadows. Wrapping her arms around her waist, she continued to walk, pacing back and forth in the darkness.

After a while a raw laugh caught in her throat. It was funny. It was crazy, ironic, and by heaven, it was funny. She had wondered how she would see Keith tonight, here in a reasonable facsimile of her world. Well, now she knew. She had looked at Keith, and she had seen the man she loved.

She *loved* him!

For most of her life she had been telling herself that love didn't exist. If parents couldn't feel love for their own child, Jenna had reasoned, then love must not exist. It was just a way of making duty and need and sexual attraction sound less ordinary.

So another myth bites the dust, she thought, dragging in a rough breath. Love existed, which meant her lifelong lie had been a defense mechanism. It had made the void in her life less personal, less painful.

And now, in the blink of an eye, the void had been filled. And it was personal. It was painful. Jenna hadn't asked for it, and now that it had found her, she didn't know what she was going to do with it.

She had known Keith for less than two weeks. Two weeks! How could it have happened so quickly? And what came next? Who provided the guidelines? Where was the book of rules? Keith had said he wanted to explore "this thing" between them. *This thing?* What in hell did that mean?

She frowned, remembering something else he had told her. Maybe they were meant to be nothing more than friends, he had said.

The idea twisted through her, adding more pain, more doubt. Ever since she had known Keith, she had seen him in a lot of different guises—gentle shepherd, dark knight, laughing guide—but after what she had just gone through, after what she had felt as she watched him with Carolyn, Jenna knew she would never be able to see him as only a friend. Never.

"You have no idea how exquisite you look in the moonlight."

The unexpected voice brought Jenna swinging abruptly around. There, in the moonlight, she saw Max, several feet away, watching her as he leaned against a low stone wall.

"I didn't know black hair could look so alive.

You've trapped pieces of light in it." He pushed away from the wall and moved toward her. "Every line of your body beckons tonight, Jenna."

She ran a hand across her face. "Not now, Max. I'm just not up to it tonight."

As though she hadn't spoken, he reached out and ran one finger down her bare arm. "Do you know what you do to me?"

She twitched her arm out of his reach. "No. And I don't want to know," she said, her voice exasperated as she turned away from him. "I'm going back in."

Grasping her arm, he spun her around to face him. "You don't know how to play the game, love. We've done the subtle, teasing looks, we've done the eager chase—now it's time for the *sauvage dénouement.*"

She drew in a deep breath. "You're obnoxious, and your ego is out of control, but I'm pretty sure that somewhere in all that muddle is an intelligent mind. Use it, for Pete's sake. *I don't want you.*"

After only the briefest hesitation he jerked her to him. "Who cares?" he said as he pressed his mouth to her neck.

For Jenna it was the final straw, the culminating bit of lunacy in a chaotic night. She saw Max through a red haze of fury as she jerked her head back, kicking him in the shin and boxing his ears in simultaneous moves.

Then, as she prepared to tell him what she thought of him in less polite terms, Max was suddenly hauled backward, away from her.

"I care," Keith said as he slung the other man toward the stone wall. "I very definitely care."

Moments later Max struggled to stand upright

and began straightening his dinner jacket, keeping his gaze away from Keith.

"You're better than this, Max," Keith said, his voice tight and low with anger. "At least you were once."

The other man's only answer was to raise his shoulders in a slight shrug before abruptly walking away.

"You know Max?" Jenna asked as she smoothed down her dress with an unsteady hand.

"Our paths crossed a few times years ago in London." He moved closer. "Did he hurt you?"

Avoiding his eyes, she gave her head a slight shake. "No, it's just annoying to have a personal decision made for me. Belittling. As though what I want and how I feel don't count."

She heard a rustling and knew he had moved again, coming closer. "I can understand that." His voice was deep and low and moved across her face and shoulders like rough moonlight. "Just because a man has greater physical strength, he has no right to grab a woman . . ."

He stood directly in front of her now, and she saw his arms rise, felt his fingers on her shoulders, digging tightly into her flesh.

". . . and haul her into his arms . . ."

He jerked her forward, catching her in his arms when she fell against him.

". . . and kiss her, whether she likes it or not."

The kiss was hard and unending. There was anger in it, anger and frustration and a hunger that was so open, so deep, it left her shaken.

"Now it's time for you to say, 'Oh no, not again,'" he whispered raggedly against her mouth.

Jenna bit at his lower lip. "Oh no, not again,"

she said obediently, then met his tongue with her own.

A rough sound came from deep in his chest, and as he wrapped his arms around her, lifting her, the satin dress moved against her skin, adding a touch of refinement to the primal embrace.

They were both breathless when the kiss ended, and he gave a choked laugh against her throat. "This damned party," he said. "When I finally got here, I couldn't reach you. I saw you, standing there, looking like every man's dream. I watched everyone in the room watching you, but I couldn't get to you. All evening there was too much space and too many people between us. Sweet heaven, Jenna, it's been a long, lonely week."

Pulling back, she met his eyes and after a moment reached up to touch his face. "You know what I was doing, don't you?"

"Oh yes," he said with a short, wry laugh. "I knew exactly what you were doing. You were trying to escape through the window, just like on your first day at kindergarten. I understood, but that didn't make waiting any less hellish. I was afraid you would make it this time."

She smoothed her palm over the side of his face to his neck, loving the feel of him. "Why did you let me hide?" she whispered. "Why didn't you come and drag me out by the hair?"

"I knew you were trying to find answers."

The words, so incredibly gentle, so unbelievably understanding, brought unexpected tears to her eyes and a little shaft of fear to her heart.

Was love an answer? she wondered. It was so *big*. Bigger and more scary than anything she had faced in her life.

"What's wrong? What are you thinking?"

She shook her head, glancing away from him. "Nothing really. Just that I had found no answers. Only more questions."

Turning her face to the moonlight, he examined her features for a long moment. "No answers? Are you sure about that?"

She drew in a slow breath and forced herself to meet his eyes. "One answer," she said. "I want to be with you. I don't know what's going to happen, but kindergarten turned out okay, so I'll take a chance. I want to spend every minute I can with you. I want to feel all those things I felt the last time we were together. And maybe I want to feel some things I didn't feel last time."

He looked suddenly paler in the moonlight. And then his eyes blazed and his hands came to her waist, digging into her flesh. "Now I drag you out by the hair," he said, his voice raspy as he whirled her around and began to move her away from the terrace.

"Jenna!"

Glancing over her shoulder, Jenna saw Dink in the open door to the great hall.

"Jenna, the band is tipsy. Every single one of them. What are we—"

"Give the fiddle to old Mr. Flaherty," Keith called back to her. "Jenna and I are going for a walk."

"Oh," Dink said, then added, "*Oh* . . . I see. Blessings on you, my children." With a wave, she went back inside.

"Where are we going?" Jenna asked.

"I don't know. Away from the lights and Max and Lady Georgiana and drunken musicians. This place has changed, but there used to be . . . yes, here it is."

At the back of Aldham Castle the surrounding wall remained only in bits and pieces. Still clasping her hand in his, Keith pulled her quickly up a circular flight of stairs and out into an open area. It was enclosed by a crumbling, shoulder-high wall and looked like a stage set from one of the eerier productions of *Hamlet*.

She turned to him to ask how he knew of this place, to ask if he had played here as a child, but before she could get the first word out, she was abruptly thrust against the wall and held there by his body.

"So you want to feel things you've never felt before?" he whispered. "I can manage that. Oh, yes, I can manage that very well."

What followed his words became some kind of alternate reality in which action and reaction were fused and her movements grew indistinguishable from his. Sound, sight, and touch—everything was thrown together in a brilliant kaleidoscope of sensation. Did the straps of her dress fall from her shoulders of their own accord? Did she feel his lips on her shoulders and breasts, or was she really feeling them in her heart? Was the rough warmth beneath her dress, the hard, rugged heat that slid inside the silk panties to cup her buttocks, was that his hands, or was the heat radiating from deep inside her? Was he lifting her, bringing her closer, fitting her body against his, or was it some sort of magnetism, some obscure law of physics that worked on its own and couldn't be stopped?

Jenna didn't know, and furthermore she didn't

care. She only knew that whatever was happening was like nothing she had ever felt before, and she wanted it to go on forever.

She wasn't sure how much time had passed before she realized Keith was speaking to her. Her head dropped back against the wall and, shaking with emotion, she closed her eyes and counted to ten. Only then did distinct words reach her.

His head lay against her bare breasts, his breathing harsh and labored. "We can't do this." When the words whispered across her flesh, she realized it wasn't the first time he had said them. "Not here. Not now," he muttered.

Pulling her straps up, he groaned as he smoothed the white satin across her breasts, then wrapped his arms around her, holding her close.

"I hope this isn't as painful for you as it is for me," he said, his voice still hoarse. "I think I went a little crazy. That's never happened before . . . something in the way you were looking at me, something in your voice—I just went crazy, Jenna. This isn't what I meant when I said we needed to explore the thing between us."

There was a hint of uneven laughter in his voice as he shook his head. "Passion as volatile as that will obscure the truth as surely as fantasies. I need to get to know you. You need to know me."

"Don't I get a vote?" Finding her voice at last, she glanced at him from beneath her lashes. "Let's— Maybe we should look at . . . um . . . our situation from a different angle. As long as we're both so . . . so tense, we won't be able to think about anything else."

He laughed and pushed a rough hand through his hair. "You like playing with fire, don't you?

Stop teasing and listen to me. I've faced up to facts that you haven't. Which means I know better what's at stake here. We're physically attracted. That's a given . . . and a hell of an understatement." He drew in a slow breath. "We have to explore the other parts."

Although Jenna still wasn't sure what had happened between them moments earlier, she had a suspicion that all her parts had been thoroughly explored, independently and in groups, but she kept her suspicions to herself.

Taking her by the shoulders, he moved her a few inches away from him. "Back to the party," he said with obvious reluctance in his voice. "When we continue this, it had better be in the bright light of day."

Part of her mind must have still been in the brilliant kaleidoscope, because they had almost reached the terrace when she placed a hand on his arm and pulled him to a halt.

"If we go back looking like this," she said, "it will cause a scandal. Here, turn around." Reaching up, she pushed the hair off his forehead, buttoned his shirt, then stood back and looked him over. "Casually elegant," she said, nodding with approval. "How about me?"

He threaded his fingers through her long hair, fluffing and rearranging, but when he began smoothing down her dress, his hands slowed, returned to her belly, then over her hips to her buttocks.

"Bad idea," he muttered, straightening away from her. "You look sexy as hell . . . like someone's been making love to you on the ramparts," he added as he took her hand and moved toward the castle.

The terrace, which had been empty when they left it, was now occupied by clusters of guests. Glancing toward them, Keith said, "I don't think I'm up to mixing and mingling. And I've had enough of watching you from across the room." He paused. "Meet me tomorrow?"

"Where?"

He smiled. "Just go for a walk. I'll find you."

When she nodded, he hesitated, as though he wanted to say something but didn't know how. Then, with a slight shrug of his shoulders, he extended his hand to her and raised his voice, "Tell Lady Georgiana and Sir Geoffrey good night for me and thank them for a wonderful evening . . . the best I've had in a very long time."

"Of course," she said, her voice polite, her lips twitching with laughter as she shook his hand.

After pulling her hand away, she stood and watched as he walked into the darkness. When he had disappeared, she glanced down and slowly opened her fingers to see what he had passed to her.

There, in Jenna's open palm, was a tiny scrap of white silk.

With an abrupt movement she raised her other hand to her hip, automatically disbelieving, and then a flood of heat rose in her cheeks and temples.

Seconds later the people milling about on the terrace turned in curiosity to stare at the raven-haired woman who stood alone, her face raised to the moonlight as she laughed aloud.

Nine

The next day Jenna went walking alone for the first time in over a week. It was still early; the sun was just breaking above the horizon, spreading soft streaks of luminescence across the dusky landscape, and there was a definite nip in the air.

She hadn't come out expecting to see Keith—he was probably birthing lambs or whatever else one did on a sheep farm at the day's beginning—but Jenna had awakened while it was still dark, and she had been too eager for the day to begin to go back to sleep. She had realized then just how much she had missed her walks through the countryside.

Pausing to lean against a tree, she looked around and smiled. Without conscious design she had made her way back to the place where she had first met Keith.

When she thought of the way he had found her, surrounded by sheep, she laughed. Then she laughed again, simply because it felt good to laugh. It felt good to be in the country on this spring morning. It felt good to be alive.

Glancing over her shoulder, she located the rocky ledge, the little rocky ledge that she had come to know so intimately on her second day in Ireland. Fairies live under that hill, he had told her. She had always thought fairies lived in green places, secluded dells or shady glens or . . .

What was a glen anyway? She didn't remember having seen any around Dallas . . . except for Glen Abernathy, her accountant, and she hoped he wasn't the shady type of glen. If he was, Jenna was in big trouble because—

Forget Glen, she told herself. This was County Limerick, and the fairies here didn't waste time on men who spent all their time talking about tax-deferred annuities. Here the fairies lived under the hills, hanging out with troglodytes, blind fish, and Tolkien.

Fairies, she thought with a wry smile. Fairies again.

What she had felt last night was real; the love that still confused her when she allowed herself to think of it, the desire that, even today, had the power to take her breath away. Those weren't temporary vacation emotions, feelings you could leave behind like wet towels on the floor of a resort motel. They were real. And last night Jenna had seen Keith the way he wanted her to see him, as a real man in the real world. But how could she keep him separate from the enchantment that permeated this land? He was a part of it all.

Turning her head slightly, she saw a man walking across the meadow toward her. And with her first glimpse of him Jenna knew she had been lying to herself again. She had known he wouldn't be birthing lambs this morning. And she hadn't come out to enjoy nature in early morning solitude. She had come out specifically to see Keith.

In that moment, as she watched him from across the field, Jenna felt a surge of love wash through her. Whoever he was, whatever he was, she loved him. Radically, thoroughly, absolutely, she loved him.

Pushing away from the tree, she ran toward him, laughing. As she drew nearer, he raised his hand, and she reached out and took it, catching her breath when he squeezed it tightly. His gaze was trained on her face with the same intensity as that first day, and in his brown eyes was the same mixture of surprise and pleasure, amusement and warm welcome.

"You found me," she said without feeling a bit silly at stating the obvious.

He laughed, a warm, rich sound that began deep in his chest, and together they turned to walk back across the meadow. Occasionally, as they talked, they would stop and face each other, becoming so involved in their conversation that they were unaware they had stopped walking.

During that day and the three that followed they spent quite a bit of time talking. There always seemed to be something that needed to be shared. Keith wanted to know about every minute of Jenna's life, just as she wanted to know about his.

She heard what it was like to be a boy on an Irish farm, what it was like to be an outsider in the dozen different places he had lived in the United States. She learned which ideas and music moved him. She got glimpses of the bruises on his soul.

She came to understand what things in the world led him to despair and what things gave him hope. She discovered he liked chocolate cake better than strawberry.

Every day, for all the daylight hours, they were together. She stayed beside him as he went about his daily work. Although they didn't birth any lambs, she saw the hard work that was involved in keeping a farm going. And then, as soon as the shadows of evening began to spread, he always took her back to Aldham Castle.

Jenna didn't have to ask why. She knew. The sensual ties that had begun forming when they first met had grown too strong. A dozen times during the day she would catch his eye and know without a doubt that he was wanting her, the same way and with the same intensity that she was wanting him. And if the attraction was that strong during the day, with all the lighted world to distract them, what would it be like when there was nothing but the sound of his voice and the feel of his hand holding hers?

Although Jenna wasn't sure what they were waiting for—what manifestation or turn of events would signal the beginning of their love affair—she knew that what they had found together was too important for them to give in to reckless need.

"Wait a minute," Jenna said, turning in the saddle to look at Keith.

They were riding across the countryside, on their way to see Duffy, whose bruised leg had been diagnosed as a cracked femur. The old man was staying with his youngest daughter and her family while he mended.

"You skipped something there," she told him. "You said a boy named Beany Baxter was teasing you about your Irish accent, then the next thing I know, you're spending a week in detention hall." She sent him a stern look. "What did you do to poor Beany?"

He grinned. "Nothing permanent. I slipped some glue under him. Which meant he either had to walk around with a lab stool stuck to his butt or to shed his jeans. That kid had the skinniest legs I've ever seen."

"Juvenile delinquent," she said, laughing with him.

A moment later he sobered and shook his head. "As a matter of fact a couple of years after that I did get mixed up with a rough crowd. Leather jackets, long hair, and bad-ass attitudes. Fortunately, before I could get into any real trouble, we moved to San Francisco." He smiled. "The juvenile delinquents in the City by the Bay were more socially conscious. There were a lot of protests— sit-ins, holding hands and singing, that kind of thing—even though most of us had no real grasp of the issues involved."

"Everything's so intense when you're a teenager," she murmured, remembering. "And you think people are lying when they tell you that the glorious mixture of angst and ecstasy is nothing more than a stage you're going through, something you'll outgrow along with your braces."

"But you don't outgrow it, not really," he said. "It's more in the way of preparation for the real thing. When you grow up, the angst and ecstasy are still there, but you don't throw them around so freely. They're in storage for you, just waiting until you meet that one cause . . . that one person."

It was there again. Without warning, without restraint, the silken threads of desire began tightening, drawing her toward him. She felt sensuality coming at her in great waves that washed through her, making her weak, and in a flashback of what she had felt on the ramparts, Jenna's breasts swelled and her flesh was electrified.

Clearing her throat, she glanced away from him. They were traveling beside a road now, a public place of sorts; it was broad daylight; and she wanted him so badly, every inch of her body ached for him.

"Get a grip," she muttered in a hoarse whisper.

"What was that?" There was a definite hint of laughter in his voice.

"Nothing, I just—"

She broke off as she recognized the car traveling along the road toward them. It was the Aldham Daimler, and as it passed, Jenna saw that Carolyn was behind the wheel, while Fiona Blair sat in the passenger seat beside her.

Although the Coombses and Ralph had left the day after the party, the Glendening-Waites were hanging on at the castle. According to Dink, even though Max was bored stiff, Carolyn kept making excuses to stay.

"I didn't know Carolyn knew Fiona," Jenna said as the car disappeared around a bend in the road.

"I didn't know you knew Fiona." He paused. "But she was at Lady Georgiana's gala, wasn't she?"

"I met her before that. At the street dance." She

shivered at the memory. "A grim sort of woman. Intense. But she seems to care a lot about you."

"Fiona and my mother grew up together. I can remember a time when she wasn't so grim, but I'm afraid life has left its imprint on her. She lost two sons in less than a month's time." He reached down to free a leaf that was caught in his stirrup. "She's Carolyn's aunt."

"Then you knew Carolyn before the party?" She didn't know why that should surprise her. He said he knew Max; it was logical that he would also know Max's wife. "You knew her as a child? I mean, you met her when she came here to visit her aunt?"

"Not visit. Fiona raised Carolyn. Yes, I knew her," he said slowly. "We played together as children. Fiona and my mother were always together."

That explained the intimacy of the scene Jenna had witnessed the night of the party and why Carolyn had looked more natural with Keith than Jenna had ever seen her. The redhead had been talking to a childhood friend.

An instant later Jenna made a choking sound. "*Carolyn* is the Lynn you've told me about? The one you always got into trouble with? The one you were skinny-dipping with when Father MacGonigal caught you?"

When he nodded, she let out a low whistle. "Carolyn," she said, her voice disbelieving. "Elegant, always perfect Carolyn. I can't picture it, but you know, it makes sense now. At first I thought she disliked me because of that awful man she's married to. He flirts right in front of her, Keith. But then I decided it was just one of those chemical things. You know, you meet someone, and for no good reason you automatically detest them. But all along it was you." She paused to consider. "I suppose there's always some possessiveness attached to a friendship. She probably feels the same as her aunt—that I'm not good enough for you."

He gave a short, rough laugh and, as though sensing tension in the air, his horse stirred beneath him. "No one in their right mind could think that."

He drew in a slow breath, his gaze on the horizon. When he spoke again, his voice was low and tight. "You have no idea, you couldn't possibly know what you've given me these last few days. It's as though all my life I've been caught in the middle of a hurricane, then suddenly, through no effort of my own, the sun comes out and there's warmth and peace all around."

The words were so damned intense, so damned genuine that they scared Jenna for a moment. But then she realized he had done the same for her. Ever since she was a little girl, she had felt as though she were standing on the edge of a precipice, blindfolded, unable to see if there was anything below to catch her if she should stumble and fall.

The blindfold was off now, and she could see that this man was beside her, holding her hand. Keith wouldn't let her fall.

As she turned to meet his dark gaze, he must have seen in her eyes the feelings she couldn't yet put into words, for in the next moment he was lifting her off her horse, pulling her into his arms to cover her mouth with his own.

"You choose the most unlikely places to decide

you want to make love to me," she said, the words low and breathy against his lips.

"There's no decision involved," he said with a hoarse laugh. "Do you think I can use my brain when you're near?" He gave his head a short, jerky shake, as though to clear it. "I don't seem to have any control over it.

"Just remember that before you look at me like that in the middle of a crowd," he muttered, then, grasping her by the waist, he lifted her back to her own horse and they continued on their way.

Briget, Duffy's daughter, was a quiet woman with laughter in her eyes, the kind of woman who had the gift of putting guests instantly at ease. After tea, which was really coffee and sandwiches, Keith went out in the yard with Briget's husband, Patrick to help him work on a defunct tractor, while Jenna stayed behind to visit with Duffy and his daughter.

After making sure her father was comfortable on a sofa in the back parlor, Briget settled down to knit, and Jenna settled down to listen to Duffy complain about not being able to work. Murmuring an occasional word of sympathy, she followed the trail of curses that touched on fate, careless assistants, and the horse that kicked him.

He was in the middle of worrying about the special vitamins Queen Mab was supposed to receive daily when Jenna happened to glance out the window. Keith had been leaning into the labyrinthine depths of the tractor motor, but as she watched, he straightened and wiped perspiration from his forehead with a white handkerchief. Although both he and Patrick had shed their shirts, Briget's husband could have been a part of the tractor for all Jenna noticed. It was Keith who held her attention. There wasn't a spare ounce of flesh on him, and the hard muscles stood out in his back and shoulders.

Why hadn't she noticed before how sexy riding pants and those tight, calf-high boots looked on a man with Keith's—

"You have an interest in tractors, do you?"

Startled, Jenna swung her gaze back to the room. Briget was no longer in the parlor, and Duffy was carefully studying Jenna's face.

"I beg your pardon?" she said.

"I was just sayin' it's rare for a woman, born and raised in the city like yourself, to show such an uncommon interest in farm equipment." He shook his head at the wonder of it. "Maybe you'd like to go out and give Patrick some instruction. He could use the help."

"No, I don't—" She broke off when she saw the twinkle in the old man's eyes, and they laughed together.

"That's a good man there," he said, sobering, "but not always an easy man to know. Sean treated Keith the way he himself was treated as a boy, never understanding his mistake. You see, Sean knew how to caution and advise, but he wasn't much of a hand at making life's blows go down easier for a boy." He shook his head. "It's queer the damage a man's pride can do him and the ones he loves."

Jenna wanted to ask questions about the divorce and about what it did to Keith, but she knew Duffy couldn't tell her what she needed to know.

He wouldn't know what was inside Keith, what scars had been left behind.

"It's time the lad was settling down."

She glanced up and found Duffy watching her again. "Do you know how the females around here have been laying traps for Keith since the day he came home? But he wouldn't look at them. Of course I knew why. Didn't he tell it to me years ago? I'm the only one, except for his father, who knew."

"Knew what? What did he tell you?"

"About the vision. About you. 'Hair black as soot, skin like fresh cream, and no bigger than could stand on the palm of your hand.' The sight is a gift from God, not for asking questions about. Keith knew none of the women around here would do for him. It had to be you and no one else."

The old man leaned forward and moved his leg to a more comfortable position. "I'm glad you've finally come, lass. Our Keith was getting lonely with the waiting."

As Jenna stared at him, the blood drained from her face, and there was a roaring sound in her ears. She rose awkwardly to her feet, her eyes wide with confusion. *Visions? The sight?*

"Duffy . . . Duffy, I just remembered something I have to do." She moistened her lips. "I don't want to bother Keith. He'll think he has to escort me home, and it's just not necessary. The castle is just over that hill back there, isn't it?" Her voice was distracted as she wiped damp palms on the sides of her riding pants. "I'll go back now. Tell Keith . . . tell him I'll see him later."

Before Duffy could do more than utter a startled "Eh?" she was gone.

At the front of the house she ran to her horse and mounted quickly. Overcoming the urge to spur the horse to speed, she made a wide circle around the house, keeping the barn between herself and where Keith worked on the tractor.

Jenna was running and she knew it, but she needed time to think. A mystical, magical love scared her. It was too fantastic and couldn't possibly last. She didn't want a brief, shining moment of Camelot. She wanted something solid and enduring, a love that would hold up to the wear and tear of everyday life.

Ordinary love, she told herself as she urged the horse up the well-worn, rocky path that cut into the wooded hill. She wanted a love that was ordinary enough to be real.

Jenna wasn't sure how much time had passed while she was brooding over what Duffy had told her, but eventually she looked around and realized the mist had come down without her noticing. She hadn't expected the mist, and the sight of it made her nervous.

It wasn't a thick mist, she assured herself. It simply obscured the horse's feet. And the trail.

A split second later something small—a rabbit, she thought—darted out across the path, and the horse, already affected by the tension in Jenna, reared back in fright. Jenna squealed and began grabbing frantically for the horse's neck. Unfortunately her reaction came too late.

The impact of hitting solid ground jolted through her body, leaving her winded, and she lay still for a moment trying to catch her breath in painful gasps. When the pain began to subside a little, she placed her hands on the damp ground and gingerly pushed herself up to a sitting position. And then she panicked.

The horse was nowhere in sight, and the mist was even thicker.

"Stay calm. Stay calm," she murmured. "Panicking never helped anything."

Cursing aloud, she wished she could forget that stupid movie she had seen about a deserted island with a perpetual mist. Everyone who got trapped on the island ended up with fungus growing all over them.

But this wasn't a deserted island and there was no perpetual mist. This was the Irish kind that would eventually disappear. What was the worst thing that could happen? She might have to spend a night in the open. She might get damp and catch a cold.

"I might have Spanish moss hanging from my arms," she muttered as she began to explore the ground with her hands.

She had landed in the grass, and although that was good news for her bones, she was no longer on the path. She didn't even know in which direction the path lay.

By moving on her hands and knees, first one way and then another, she managed to find a rocky stretch and assured herself that it was the path and not some other rocky stretch. Rising to her feet, she began to move slowly through the mist. Whenever she felt something other than rock beneath her feet, she would stoop and again use her hands to locate the trail. It was tedious, and her boots were definitely not made for walking, but at least she felt as though she were doing something.

It was so weird, she told herself. She was out in

the open, but with the mist all around her she felt closed in, claustrophobic, and each breath felt strangely muffled.

A moment later she abruptly stopped walking. In worrying about how difficult it was to breathe, she had stopped paying attention to the trail and now felt the softness of grass under her boots again.

With a little whimper, she stooped and began to feel the ground with shaking fingers. She couldn't have wandered far from the path. She couldn't have.

A moment later her left hip bumped into something solid, and she went stock-still. Whatever it was felt hard and cold. Not soft and alive, thank God. Moving just a little, she felt the thing with her hands. When she began to trace an indecipherable pattern with one finger, she was sure she had found a gravestone, that she had somehow managed to wander into a graveyard, but while still trying to cope with the distressing idea, the truth came to her. It was a Celtic cross, one of the thousands that dotted the Irish countryside.

"This is good," she told herself aloud. "This is good. Even if the mist decides to be perpetual, some stupid tourist will eventually come up here to take a picture. And then I'll be found."

With a shaky laugh she moved to sit with her back to the cross, taking comfort from it. This monument had been carved from a granite boulder by dedicated, caring people. It would bring her luck.

After a while she shifted her position and glanced around. Yup, the mist was still as thick as ever, she told herself, and wondered if she should start singing.

When Jenna was a little girl, her parents had occasionally left her alone at night, telling her that she was a big girl and could stay by herself for a few hours, even if it was dark outside. She would watch them leave, then go to her room, sit in the corner and sing to herself until they came back. There had been times when she had sung herself hoarse.

She would feel silly doing the same thing now. She was a grown woman, and grown women didn't—

After she finished singing about the dog named Bingo, she gave a vigorous rendition of "Show Me the Way to Go Home," then started on the beer bottles. There were only sixteen bottles of beer left on the wall when, directly in front of her, the mist swirled, and a misty, moisty man-shape appeared. Keith.

A sound that was something between a sob and a laugh caught in her throat as she surged to her feet and threw herself into his arms.

"Hush, alanna, hush now," he soothed, holding her tightly. "Didn't you know I would find you? I'll always find you, Jenna."

"I wasn't afraid," she said, her voice hoarse from singing. "I knew the mist would disappear eventually. I knew all I had to do was— God, I was so scared, Keith. It was a stupid thing to do. Totally, completely *stupid*. When I get lost in Dallas, I just stop at a 7–11 or a Texaco station and . . . It might be better if you slap me now. I think I'm getting hysterical."

He laughed and held her even tighter. "You're

fine. And so am I . . . now. I have to admit, when I saw your horse at the bottom of the hill, I came close to hysterics myself. But I knew I would find you." Dropping a hand to her waist, he turned her. "Are you up to a walk? There's a hut just across the way here. We can build a fire, and before you know it, we'll be warm and dry."

It sounded like heaven. Although she didn't see how he was going to find his way through the fog, she trusted him. So, with one hand in his and the other clutching his shirt sleeve for extra protection, she let him lead her.

Half an hour later, as promised, she was warm, and her clothes were almost dry. Glancing around the cabin, she took in the lantern sitting on a wooden table. A narrow cot was shoved against one wall. There were two chairs at the table and some sort of wooden cabinet by the door. That was the extent of the furnishings.

Turning her head slightly, she found Keith watching her. "Ready to talk?" he asked quietly.

She moistened lips that had suddenly gone dry. "I don't know. Probably not, but that's because I'm a coward. I guess now is as good a time as any."

Moving away from the fire, she kept her back to him, then after a moment she glanced over her shoulder. "Did Duffy tell you what we were talking about before I left?"

He nodded. "He told me. How do you feel about it?"

A short laugh escaped her. "How am I supposed to feel? I thought we were supposed to be getting to know each other, but why should we? I mean, if this"—she waved a hand between them—"is pre-arranged, if our fates have been woven together on some cosmic loom, what difference does it make what I'm like or what you're like?"

She drew in an unsteady breath. "You told me I didn't see you, that I was making you up to fit into my vacation dream. But all the time you were . . . You said we couldn't let fantasies, *yours or mine*, get in the way. Why didn't I catch that? Why didn't I ask what you meant?"

Turning, she moved a step toward him. "When we met, did you see *me*, or did you see the woman in the vision? You forced me to see you as a real man, but in all the time we've spent together, have you ever seen *me*?"

He gave a harsh laugh. "I saw you. God, yes, I saw you. I couldn't see anyone but you." He pushed a hand through his hair. "I know the idea will take some getting used to. Judas priest, don't you think it gave me problems too? But what you've got to understand, what *I've* come to understand, is that the vision doesn't matter. The past, the future, nothing counts except what we feel when we're together. I don't care if all the angels in heaven got together and chose you for me and me for you. What matters is that *I chose you* . . . and I hope you'll choose me as well."

She shook her head, slowly at first, then with growing emphasis. "You're doing it again. You're feeding me fairy tales and at the same time telling me to get real. You can't have it both ways."

"I can." He grasped her shoulders to give her a small shake. "*You* can. I've seen you separate things—emotions and experiences and people—into neat little pockets in your mind. That's what you're doing now. You're putting magic into one pocket and reality into another. I'm telling you to merge the two. Believe that the magic we have between us is real. The magic is the love . . . and don't try to tell me you don't love me. I've seen it in your face, just as surely as you've seen it in mine. The love between us is magic, Jenna . . . and the magic is real."

She heard the words, she even heard the ring of truth in them, but they didn't make sense to her. Not yet. She was still caught up in an alternate truth, one she had learned a long time ago: Fairies and elves were for children, there was no such thing as unqualified love, and miracles stopped happening the day the world grew up.

Keith watched expressions play across Jenna's lovely face, recognizing the resentment in her violet eyes, but resentment wasn't the only thing he saw there. He saw fear. And he saw a deep yearning there, a yearning to believe.

There were things he wanted so badly to give her, but he knew he couldn't. What he wanted to give her was something she could only find for herself.

"I can't force you to believe that the good things exist. The magical things. Faith . . . hope . . . love. They have no shape or form. You can't hold faith or hope in your hands. You can't look at love through a microscope. But it would be a poor sort of world if they didn't exist."

Unclenching his fists, he tried to ease the desperation from his voice. "Each of us is given a choice, Jenna. You can believe . . . or not. The choice is up to you. No scientific test will help. And you can't use logic. You can't even use your own senses. You have to use your heart," he whispered softly. "If you just once believe in the unbelievable, the world will never be the same place. Believe in it just once, and all things are possible."

Jenna pushed the hair from her forehead with an unsteady hand. He made it sound simple. He made it sound right and rational. But it wasn't. Self-protection was a lesson Jenna had learned long ago, and she knew all about faith, hope, and love. Faith was a wisp of smoke that floated through the fingers of anyone trying to grasp it. Hope was nothing more than a panacea, the last resort of those who had lost everything else. And love . . . The kind of love he was talking about, the heart-touching-heart kind of love, opened the gates and allowed pain to come in.

Glancing up, she met his eyes and knew he was silently asking her to believe the impossible. She wanted to. Sweet heaven, she wanted to more than she had ever wanted anything, but she didn't know if she could.

Moving back to the fireplace, she gazed into the flames and thought of how, in times past, females in China lived their whole lives with their feet stunted by cloth bindings. She had heard that unwrapping the feet of a grown woman would bring unendurable pain. Unendurable pain.

"Jenna."

She heard the whispered word, felt the hand on her shoulder, then he was swinging her around to face him. When he placed his hands on either side of her face, it wasn't a gentle touch. She could feel the urgency in his hard palms and knew he was dealing with his own brand of pain.

"Believe," he told her, the words tight and low. "Believe in me. *Believe in us.*"

She continued to stare at him without speaking.

But somehow he knew. He knew that he had finally loosened the bindings on her heart. Inside that stunted organ was her innocence. Inside was a child who still believed in the magic of faith, hope, and love.

"God, don't tremble so," he said, his fingers tightening on her face. "I'll have a care, Jenna. I won't let harm reach you. I make the promise now and forever: "I'll have a care."

A breathless sob caught at the back of her throat, and then she was in his arms.

There were no more words. After three days of nonstop conversation, there were no more words. Because words weren't necessary. They were talking with their lips, with their hands, with their bodies.

Now that she believed, Jenna was reckless with her need, and she felt the shock of that reckless need jolt through him. A groan came from deep in his chest, and he scooped her up into his arms and carried her to the narrow cot.

He lay beside her, then was touching her in a way no man had touched her before. He was touching the very heart of her. Here, in this small cabin, surrounded by mist, she was finally finding the emphatic love she had yearned for all her life.

She felt him trying to slow the pace of their desire, trying to be cautious for her sake. He eased the clothes from her body, taking care that there were no sudden, jarring movements.

But Jenna wouldn't have it. She was starving for him, wild for him. She took off her bra and panties and, with no thought of modesty, pressed her body against his, desperate for the feel of his body against hers.

When Keith pulled away from her to strip off his clothes, he stood for a moment beside the cot and stared down at her body. The pale skin, the midnight hair lying in a tangle across the rough blanket, made his heart jerk in reaction, then pick up a frantic pace. Now that all was right between them, now that it was time for the next step, he let his feelings for her have free reign, and the power of them tightened around his chest like a vise.

He was shaking all over when he knelt beside her, moving an unsteady hand across her body as he whispered his need to her. Such a small woman, but so perfect for him. Thank God, he had finally found her.

Jenna caught her breath and dug her fingers into the rough blanket when she felt his hard thighs slide between hers. It was almost funny. The rational thought she had always valued so highly was somewhere else tonight. She didn't worry about yesterday or tomorrow. She gave no thought to the rest of the world. She could think only of what it felt like to have this man inside her, filling her, forcefully assuaging her tremendous, aching need.

Each movement, each whispered word, each insistent stroke of his hand, struck deep, and she felt the effect all the way to her soul. As they moved together, the light from the lantern added a soft glow to the urgently entwined flesh on the narrow cot.

And then Jenna felt it build inside her. She didn't know what it was, this unfamiliar force, but she knew it was essential, and she fought for it. The wildness of it caught her up and urged her on. Moments later it was close enough for her to touch. It was in her and in him. The piercingly sweet sensations filled her completely, bonding her soul to his and leaving her with peace.

Keith lay with his hand on her breasts, his breath coming in harsh drafts. Then, sensing something in her, he moved his hand to her warm throat.

"What is it, love?" he said in a rough whisper, and in his own voice he heard gratitude. He heard love.

Raising his head, he looked deep into her eyes, and what he saw there made him want to cry. He was a grown man and he wanted to cry because something so beautiful, something so wonderful as this woman had come his way.

"I think I know what you're feeling," he whispered. "You're thinking this doesn't happen. It simply doesn't happen." He heard the unsteadiness in his own voice and swallowed heavily. "And yet it did. It happened for us. How could you have not believed?"

Jenna reached up to touch his face. She didn't understand it herself. Because now she knew that this was meant to be. Something larger than chance had brought them together. Her whole life had been leading her to Keith's arms.

The enchantment was real, she told herself as she wrapped her arms more tightly around him. And once every century or so, miracles still happened.

Ten

Keith helped Jenna off her horse and held her close for a moment. "Go on in the house and take that nice hot bath you've been whining about for the last two hours while I go off and do manly things, like telling one of the lads to take care of the horses."

Although the day was well along, they were only just now returning to Donegal Farm. Neither of them had wanted to leave the hut on the hill, and they had used up more time when Jenna demanded that they stop by the Celtic cross so she could see what it looked like without the fog. Later, at Briget's house, where they had stopped to collect the horses, Jenna had called Dink to let her know both she and Keith were alive and well.

In fact I've never been more alive or more well, she told herself silently now. And the credit for that went to the man beside her.

Reaching up, she gave Keith's cheek a small

pat. "There's something so virile about a man who knows how to give orders."

He turned her toward the house and swatted her on the behind. "And don't dawdle in your bath," he called after her. "A farmer's wife has to manage her time."

Jenna laughed, loving the sound of those words, and went inside, shouting hello to his housekeeper as she ran up the stairs.

Minutes later, in the old-fashioned tub, she rested her head against the porcelain and sighed as hot water and tiny soap bubbles stroked her body. Only now did she pause to take stock of the changes in herself.

She could see some of the changes, she thought, as she ran a hand down her body. Her curves seemed softer and more womanly. But the other changes, the ones in her mind and heart, were the most important. Her heart and mind were also softer, and open to any wonder the world had to offer.

With only a little effort, she decided lazily, she could believe that all of history had taken place simply to bring her and Keith together. Eons ago, when the first organism, upon realizing how dull it was simply to sit around dividing into more organisms, had looked around for a like-minded glob to mate with; when the first squishy creature crawled out of the sea and walked on land; when the first hairy little beast decided to stand upright; when the first man fashioned a tool and used it to plant wheat: it all happened just so one lost woman could find one wonderful man. The world had been invented so that Jenna could finally come home where she belonged.

With a small frown she realized that her own insecurity had been one of the biggest stumbling blocks to accepting what she and Keith were to each other. And in truth, it still gave her a few twinges if she allowed it. Perfect things didn't happen to imperfect people. At least that's what she used to think, she assured herself as she lazily soaped her arm. She knew differently now.

And perhaps that was Keith's greatest triumph. He had made her see that, in one man's eyes, she was extraordinary. She was special enough for a miracle.

After changing into the sweater and jeans that Mrs. Kennedy had provided, clothes Keith had worn as a boy, Jenna ran downstairs again, eager to show off the bulky sweater and baggy jeans, and even more eager to be in his arms again. When she didn't find him in the house, she left by the back door and made her way toward the stables.

She was rounding the north corner of the barn when she saw him. His back was to her, and facing him was a woman with brilliant red hair. Carolyn.

". . . know very well what you're doing, don't think I don't," Carolyn was saying. "You're using her to put a barrier between us because of your stupid *honor*." She made the word sound vulgar. "I know you hate the fact that I'm married, but I've told you it means nothing. *Nothing*. It would take more than Max and that black-haired witch to break the hold we have on each other. No law, of God or man, can do that. And certainly not your miserable little American! Since the first time we made love, Keith, I knew it would always be the two of us. I *knew* it. Just as you knew."

"Does Max know as well?" Keith's voice was almost inaudible, making Jenna wish she could see his face. She needed to see his dark eyes. She would read the truth in his eyes, and then she would know that these words, words that were slicing into her heart through her, were all lies.

Carolyn made a short sound of contempt. "Max is useless. Surely you're not jealous of him." She moved closer and rested a hand on his chest. "Remember all those nights in London? You weren't worried about Max then. I go weak just thinking of them." Her voice had grown husky. "I need you, Keith. I know you said we couldn't be seen together on Donegal Farm, but— No wait, listen to me. If we can't be together here, come back to London with me. You still have clothes at the apartment and you can—"

Keith said something that Jenna couldn't hear, words that were low and intense.

"No!" The redhead's face had tightened into an angry mask as he spoke. "You *can't* be with her. I won't let you. It's that stupid old man, still haunting you. You're buying into your father's vision. Your *father's* dream!" she accused.

His father's dream? Jenna's hands tightened into fists as her heart began to beat at a frantic pace. She was lying. *Damn it, Keith, call her a liar,* she pleaded silently.

"You're ruining both our lives because you feel guilty," Carolyn spat out at him. "I can remember what Sean looked like when he found out about us. God, that old man hated me. Don't you understand? That's why he reminded you about the woman he said you were meant to marry. Are you going to deny the slut is exactly as your father said she would be? I remember every word." She gave a harsh laugh. "Will I ever forget? 'Hair as black as soot, skin like cream, and no bigger than could stand on the palm of your hand.' We laughed at it! Don't you remember that, how you and I used to laugh at his stupid vision? The woman who'll love you true. The woman whose love will be given only to you."

Jenna's vision blurred as the words scraped down her skin with red-hot prongs.

"Your simpering Jenna was a virgin, wasn't she?" Carolyn continued, her voice filled with hatred. "No, you don't have to answer. I know you've convinced yourself that your father had the sight, but he was just a crazy old man, and the black-haired bitch is nothing more than a coincidence! A *stupid coincidence*. He said she was the only one who would do for your wife, but she was *his* choice, darling. Not yours. Doesn't it make you angry that you're preparing to base your entire future on a dream that's not even your own? The old vulture is dead now. For God's sake, let his fairy tale die with him. He deserves no respect from you. Why should you—"

Jenna swayed just a little, but it was enough to draw Carolyn's attention to her. When the red-head broke off and glanced over Keith's shoulder, he stiffened and swung around on his heel.

Jenna couldn't see Keith's face. Pain was squeezing the life from her, and she couldn't see him. She couldn't hear or think. She could only run.

Although she didn't remember which direction

she should take to get back to the castle, it didn't matter. She only wanted to get away. From Carolyn. From Keith. From the incredible, ripping pain.

She hadn't gone far before she felt a hand on her arm, pulling her to a stop, jerking her around so sharply, she almost fell. And when he tried to pull her into his arms, Jenna shook her head wildly, slapping at his hands to make him let her go.

"Don't . . . don't . . . no! Leave me alone," she gasped as she backed away from him. "You can't—I won't have you—"

"Shhh . . . you're crying too hard to make sense," he said, his voice low and soothing. "Jenna, please. Will you listen to me?"

"Oh no, not again," she said through clenched teeth. "Not again. You lie. Sweet heaven, how you lie." Wrapping her arms around her waist, she bent over with pain. "You made me believe. You made me *believe*."

She waved a hand in the direction of the farmhouse. "You didn't say a word to refute her. But you couldn't, could you? She was telling the truth. That's why you recognized me. That's why you chased me. Not your vision. *His*. You're trying to use me to appease your guilt. In marrying me you would finally be doing something your father approved of."

She closed her eyes to shut out the sight of him. "You made me feel special. You made me feel *loved*." The last word came out in a broken whisper. "Lies, all of it. Even the part about you and Carolyn. Buddies, you said. Childhood friends. You didn't tell me that you're lovers."

"Were. *Were* lovers," he corrected, his voice hard and stiff. "It was a long time ago."

"I feel *so damn stupid!* I knew there was something. The way she watched you. The way you avoided her. I *knew* there was something. But I was so caught up in miracles and leprechauns, I didn't have time to worry about anything else."

She raised her head and met his eyes. "I hate you for this, Keith. I hate you for making . . ." Her voice dropped to a tight whisper. ". . . for making me feel those things."

Then she turned and walked away. She heard him call her name once, but she didn't look back.

When Jenna reached the castle, she went in through a side door and straight up to her bedroom. Pulling her bags from the closet, she began scooping clothes from the bureau and dumping them carelessly into the leather cases.

She had an armload from the closet when the door swung open violently, crashing loudly against the wall.

After taking one look at the man in the doorway, she glanced frantically around for an escape route. But there was nowhere to run.

"Don't even think about the window," he said, his voice low and tight. "You won't make it."

He was the dark knight again. And he was angry as hell.

"What kind of hit-and-run game was that?" He moved into the room. "Maybe you don't want to hear my explanation, but you're going to. You're going to listen to every word, if I have to tie you to the bed to make you stay put."

"First, Lynn." As he moved forward, Jenna moved backward, away from him. "I told you how we ran wild together when we were kids. What I didn't tell you was that I met her again right after college, in London. I'm not proud of what happened, and it's not something I talk about." He met her eyes as she backed into the wall. "I didn't know she was married, Jenna. I swear I didn't know."

He paused and pushed a rough hand through his hair. "I don't think I have to justify every relationship I've had in my life, and I don't want to take anything away from Lynn, but I'm going to tell you this so you'll understand. I had been in exile for more than ten years. *Ten years.* I ached for my home. Can you understand that? And then I met Lynn at a party. She was a piece of home. A symbol of my life, back when it was simpler. Happier. Before my mother—Before my father forced me to choose between them."

He drew in a slow breath. "Yes, Lynn and I had an affair. It lasted several months. But you see, even before I found out about Max, I knew I was using her. I was making her a substitute for what I really wanted. I wanted to come home," he said simply. "But Lynn wasn't home. She was a beautiful, intelligent woman who deserved better than what I could give her."

He shook his head. "Maybe I should have told you, I don't know. I just don't know. Try to put yourself in my place for a minute. Lynn was hurt by what I did. It hurt that I couldn't love her, and it hurt that I wouldn't stay with her without loving her. She wanted to divorce Max for me, and I—I had to tell her that even if she were free, we couldn't be together. I had to tell her I didn't want her, Jenna. It was humiliating for her, and if the situation were reversed, I wouldn't want her talking about it. It was over and best forgotten."

"*It wasn't over!*" Jenna said through tight, bloodless lips. "It wasn't forgotten. She's still in love with you. And you didn't say one damn word about it to me."

"I made a freakin' mistake!" he ground out. "Okay? I made a mistake. I met her soon after she arrived here and I realized she was still . . . hoping. She thought that my father's death might make a difference. But don't you see? I had just met you. It was the day after the fair, and already I knew I was falling in love with you. But we had only known each other for *two days*. What was I supposed to do? Should I have said, 'The woman is chasing me. Make her stop'?"

"Later," she whispered. "You could have said something later."

He moved his shoulders in a restless shrug. "I thought I had made my position clear to her. I thought I had handled it."

Jenna didn't know what to think, what to feel, and suddenly she was very tired. "Even—even if what you say is true, that doesn't explain the rest," she said, her voice weary. "You made me believe in something you didn't even believe in yourself. I believed that, because of *your* vision, something bigger than chance had brought us together. And you let me believe that. You encouraged me to believe in a lie."

He swung away from her in a frustrated movement. "I didn't know you thought it was my vision. I thought Duffy had told you the whole story. My father told me about it when I was only eight. He said he had seen the woman I would love for my entire life. The woman who would love me true. Back then I thought it was a fairy tale, and I got it all mixed up with Queen Brianna. Then later—"

"Later you laughed," she said quietly.

"No!" he said, turning back to face her. "I never laughed. Lynn laughed. But I'm too much the Irishman to laugh at something like that."

He shook his head. "Lynn showed up one day at Donegal Farm, about three years ago. The affair was long over, but Da was never slow. He knew there was more between us than friendship. I'll never forget the look on his face. When she left, he didn't say a word about her. He simply reminded me of the woman he had seen in the vision so many years before."

Shoving his hands into his pockets, he dropped his gaze to the floor. "Then last year he died." The words were blunt and without emotion. "And I forgot again. Until the day I found you in the meadow. I thought it was some kind of wild coincidence. A little joke life had decided to play on me. And then—I don't know, Jenna. Maybe I wanted to get to know you better because subconsciously I wanted to please my father."

He raised his head and met her eyes. "But one thing I'm sure of—I fell in love with you. On my own, with no help from Da, no help from fate or destiny, no help from anyone. I didn't know . . . I never knew there was a great black abyss in my life until you came along and filled it. I'm whole when I'm with you, Jenna."

She couldn't stand it. She couldn't stand looking into his eyes and seeing the desperate need there. Swinging away from him, she placed a hand on the cold glass of the window and stared down into the courtyard with unseeing eyes.

She knew when he came to stand directly behind her. Even if she hadn't felt his heat, she would have known.

"There was no one else involved last night when we made love," he said in a raspy whisper. "There were no thoughts of visions or destiny when I held you, naked, in my arms. Were you thinking of fate when I caught your moan in my mouth and made your pleasure a part of mine?"

She stepped away from him, one hand pressed to her heart to still it. "What—" She broke off and cleared her throat. "Do you get some kind of kick out of manipulating me? You made me fall in love with you. You made me expose every soft place, body and soul, then you turn around and touch a hot iron to them."

When her lips trembled, she clenched her fists and held her head higher. "You promised to have a care, Keith, but it was just another lie."

He stood quietly studying her face. The anger was gone in him now. He simply looked tired, tired to death.

"You're wrong," he said without heat, without inflection. "You've made two big mistakes in your thinking. You said I didn't believe in the inevitability of our love, and two weeks ago you would have been right about that. Do you know when I began to believe, Jenna? The first time I kissed you, there on the blanket beside the river. That's when I knew the truth. I looked into your eyes and I knew that you were the only woman I would ever love. Your second mistake is thinking that you ever believed in our love. If you really believed, you'd be trying to work this out. But you're not, are you? You're running away again."

He turned and began moving toward the door. "And this time, alanna, I won't be chasing after you."

And then he was gone.

Jenna was still staring at the spot where he had stood when Dink appeared in the doorway.

Glancing at the open bags on the bed, her friend said, "You okay?"

Jenna shrugged her shoulders and turned back to her packing.

"Where are you going now?" Dink asked after a moment.

Pushing a hand through her hair, Jenna gave a broken laugh and said, "Bora Bora."

She made it as far as London. At a little hotel outside the city Jenna finally found the peace and quiet Dr. Weston had prescribed for her. The Other Symptom visited her during her first sleepless nights, but after that she had wandered through miles and miles of streets alone, physically exhausting herself, and the voices left her alone.

A couple of days of numbness passed before Jenna began to feel again, and it was a painful reawakening. Then finally the pain eased enough for her to call up the things Keith had said to her in her bedroom at the castle.

She went over every word he said, every expression on his face, every inflection of his voice. Although the memory brought back more of the pain, she dealt with it.

She had been in London for more than a week before she felt strong enough to call Dink at Aldham Castle.

"Max left," Dink said moments after coming on the line.

"Max? What about Carolyn?"

"She's staying with Fiona. To tell you the truth, I think she and Max split." She paused. "Is something going on between Keith and Carolyn? Is that why you left?"

"What makes you ask that?" Jenna asked, her voice sharp. "Have you seen them together?"

There was another pause. "No . . . no, I haven't. But there was something in your voice just now, and there was something in Keith's expression when I asked him—"

"Damn it, Dink, have you been butting into my business again?"

"Don't yell. I'm too close to labor for yelling. I haven't been butting in. The man's a neighbor. I simply paid a neighborly call. It's what nobility does, for heaven's—Okay, I was butting in, but someone needs to. He's hurting, Jeebo."

Jenna's fingers tightened on the receiver. "You think I'm not?"

"Can't you patch it up?"

She drew in a shaky breath. "I don't know. I'm not sure. I think I may have acted stupidly."

"He would understand that. I mean, acting stupid is one of the things you do. It's a little personality quirk, that's all. Anyone who loves you understands that."

Anyone who loves you, Jenna thought later as she walked through the hotel's carefully tended garden. *Anyone who loves you.*

Jenna walked slowly across the meadow, keeping her gaze trained on the farmhouse in the distance. She had dumped her bags at the castle, told Dink she would explain later, and set out.

She had spent the previous night sitting in a straight-backed chair, thinking. The result was a measure of understanding about herself and her motives. All her life Jenna had been holding on to hurt. It was a thing she did well. But now she understood that holding on to hurt was just another way of giving up. It was just another window she could escape through when she was afraid.

Now that she understood, now that she knew all of the truth, Jenna had to explain it all to Keith. And she prayed he would understand as well.

She was only a few yards away from the front door when Carolyn walked around the corner of the house and moved toward a small black car.

Spotting Jenna, the redhead stopped in her tracks. "What are you doing here? I thought you had gone for good."

Jenna counted to ten, then said, "I didn't know I was supposed to pass out my itinerary. Is Keith here?"

Carolyn moved closer. "Leave him alone. As soon as my divorce is final, Keith and I will be married. He loves me, you know. He has always loved me . . . and he will until the day he dies. So, you see, there's no need for you to hang around here trying to make him feel sorry for you."

"If he loves you so much," Jenna said slowly, "why are you bothering to warn me off? Men don't dump the love of their lives to be with someone they pity."

Before the last words were out of her mouth, the redhead struck Jenna with an open hand across the face.

Jenna counted to twenty this time. With a slight smile she shook her head. "First your husband manhandles me, now you. If you want to get tag team going, I'm one man short."

The redhead stood there for a moment, shaking with anger, then she swung abruptly around, got into the car, and drove away, leaving a cloud of dust to settle around Jenna.

When the car was out of sight, Jenna turned back toward the house, then stopped in her tracks. Keith was standing not three feet away, watching her. He wore work clothes—faded jeans and a blue, oil-stained work shirt with the sleeves rolled up, revealing his forearms.

Sliding her damp palms over her slacks, Jenna let her lips curve upward in a crooked smile. "I'm back," she said inadequately.

"So I see. Why didn't you hit her back?"

She shrugged. "It would have degenerated, and we would have been rolling around in the dirt." She shrugged again. "A fight would have done a lot for my temper but nothing at all for my dignity, and I need all the dignity I can get right now."

After staring at her for a moment longer, he turned away and walked around the corner, out of sight. It might have been her imagination, but he didn't seem overly impressed by the fact that she was back.

She found him in the side yard, cleaning a small motor with a gasoline-soaked rag.

"Need any help?" she asked as she came up to him.

His movements stilled, then without looking up, he said, "What are you doing, Jenna?"

"I told you. I'm back."

"For how long?"

He was hurt, really hurt, and the fact that she had given him so much pain twisted through her like a knife.

She stared at her hands for a moment. "I realize now why it hurt so much to find out about Carolyn," she said quietly. "You had a choice. You could hurt her by talking or hurt me by your silence. You chose her."

Straightening with an abrupt movement, he threw a wrench against the barn door with force, then turned to her, his eyes blazing. "I didn't *choose* her . . . at least not the way you mean. You don't have a clue, do you? You don't give charity to a millionaire, Jenna. You give it to the beggar on the street. You don't give a helping hand to the runner who's winning the race. You give it to the guy who's fallen flat on his face. I 'chose' Lynn, as you put it, because she deserved my pity. She'll never have what you have, not if she lives a thousand lifetimes. You have charm and wit and beauty. You're vibrant and alive. You glow from inside. You draw people to you like a fire on a cold day."

He gave a harsh laugh. "All this time you've spent disbelieving in love, did you ever stop to look around you? Everyone loves you. It's the easiest thing in the world to love you."

Raising her gaze from her hands, she said, "Everyone loves me?"

He met her eyes for a split second, then turned away from her. "I need someone who will stay for the long haul," he said, his voice flat, the words abrupt. "I can't always be wondering if the next fight is going to be the one that will cause you to leave again."

Something in his voice, something in his stiff back, got through to her, and suddenly she was scared to death. "What about your father's vision?" she said through lips gone dry with panic. "He saw me. He knew I was the one for you."

His laugh was choked off before it began. "And you hated that, didn't you? You must really be desperate to use it now."

"Yes," she admitted. "I'm desperate. Desperate enough to use the stupid vision. But the fact that I resented it doesn't make it any less real."

"He's gone now. I loved him, but I won't let him force any more impossible choices on me."

Jenna stood for a moment, helplessly watching him in silence. Now was the time for her to leave. He had told her that he didn't trust her, that he didn't care to put his love in her keeping. It was time for her to walk away and work at getting over the pain of losing him.

So why wasn't she leaving?

Moving a couple of feet away, she sat down on a stump and began plucking lint from her slacks.

There was an exasperated noise from somewhere behind her, and another tool hit the barn door. "Judas priest, what are you doing now?"

"I'm not sure, but I think I'm hanging in there. It's a difficult thing to recognize because I've never done it before. I gave up on my relationship with my parents, I gave up on my art career, I gave up on my fiancé. None of them . . . not one of them ever said, flat out, 'Go,' like you did. When it got just a little tough, I would give up and run for cover. I never had as much reason to turn and run as I do now. And I'm still here." She glanced over her shoulder at him and shook her head. "Go figure it."

He swung away, his fists clenched, then swung back to face her. "You can't do this, Jenna."

"Yes, I can," she said quietly. "I'm already doing it. You said you wouldn't let your father force another impossible choice on you, but that's what you're trying to do to me. Well, I won't let you do it. You can't make me go when I've made the decision to stay."

She stood up, anger rising in her now. "I'm not the one who's giving up when things get tough. You're doing that. The thing is, we both made mistakes. You didn't tell me about Carolyn, and I ran away. So now we're even."

"*Even*? You think we're even?" His eyes were wide with disbelief. "Not hardly. There was only one Lynn in my life. How many times will you change your mind?"

"So I'm squirrelly!" she shouted, leaning toward

him. "You knew that. You knew before you fell in love with me. Four times since I met you, I've run away. But I always come back. Doesn't that count for anything." Wiping the tears from her cheeks, she moved a step closer. "Am I not allowed one little character flaw? Do I have to be perfect to be worthy of your love?"

Grasping her arms, he gave her a hard shake, then pulled her roughly into his arms. "One little character flaw? Do you know what it does to me when you leave? Saying it's only a little flaw is like cutting off a man's hand and telling him it's only a little mistake. Don't you see? When you leave me, I bleed to death. How can I spend the rest of my life in cold sweat, constantly afraid of losing you?"

"I'm here. Will you listen to me?" She touched his face with trembling fingers. "I'm here to stay. For good. For always. I love you, Keith. It would be nice if you could accept that now, but if you can't, it won't change anything. I'll still be here. That's what I found out during this past week. No matter what happens, no matter how many times I get hurt, even if there were a dozen Carolyns in your life, it's still worth it. Loving you is worth it. Can you match that?"

His arms tightened around her with such urgency that she could barely breathe.

"Look at me," she whispered. "Then tell me what you see in my eyes."

"My life," he said, the words rough and barely audible.

Then as he looked deeper, the pain left his dark eyes and wonder began to take its place. "You believe," he said, holding her face between his hands. "You really believe this time."

With a laugh of pure joy, he scooped her up in his arms and carried her into the house and up the stairs. Jenna was home. Home was this man's arms, and this time she was in them to stay.

THE EDITOR'S CORNER

There's a lot to look forward to from LOVESWEPT in October—five fabulous stories from your favorites, and a delightful novel from an exciting new author. You know you can always rely on LOVESWEPT to provide six top-notch—and thrilling—romances each and every month.

Leading the lineup is Marcia Evanick, with **SWEET TEMPTATION**, LOVESWEPT #570. And sweet temptation is just what Augusta Bodine is, as Garrison Fisher soon finds out. Paleontologist Garrison thinks the Georgia peach can't survive roughing it in his dusty dinosaur-fossil dig—but she meets his skepticism with bewitching stubbornness and a wildfire taste for adventure that he quickly longs to explore . . . and satisfy. Marcia is at her best with this heartwarming and funny romance.

Strange occurrences and the magic of love are waiting for you on board the **SCARLET BUTTERFLY,** LOVESWEPT #571, by Sandra Chastain. Ever since Sean Rogan restored the ancient—and possibly haunted—ship, he'd been prepared for anything, except the woman he finds sleeping in his bunk! The rogue sea captain warns Carolina Evans that he's no safe haven in a storm, but she's intent on fulfilling a promise made long ago, a promise of love. Boldly imaginative, richly emotional, **SCARLET BUTTERFLY** is a winner from Sandra.

Please give a big welcome to new author Leanne Banks and her very first LOVESWEPT, **GUARDIAN ANGEL,** #572. In this enchanting romance Talia McKenzie is caught in the impossible situation of working very closely with Trace Barringer on a charity drive. He'd starred in her teenage daydreams, but now there's bad blood between their families. What is she to do, especially when Trace wants nothing less from her than her love? The answer makes for one surefire treat. Enjoy one of our New Faces of 1992!

Ever-popular Fayrene Preston creates a blazing inferno of desire in **IN THE HEAT OF THE NIGHT,** LOVESWEPT #573. Philip Killane expects trouble when Jacey finally comes home after so many years, for he's never forgotten the night she'd branded him with her fire, the night that had nearly ruined their lives. But he isn't prepared for the fact that his stepsister is more gorgeous than ever . . . or that he wants a second chance. An utterly sensational romance, with passion at its most potent—only from Fayrene!

In Gail Douglas's new LOVESWEPT, **THE LADY IS A SCAMP,** #574, the lady in the title is event planner Victoria Chase. She's usually poised and elegant, but businessman Dan Stewart upsets her equilibrium. Maybe it's his handshake that sets her on fire, or the intense blue eyes that see right inside her soul. She should be running to the hills instead of straight into his arms. This story showcases the winning charm of Gail's writing—plus a puppet and a clown who show our hero and heroine the path to love.

We end the month with **FORBIDDEN DREAMS** by Judy Gill, LOVESWEPT #575. When Jason O'Keefe blows back into Shell Landry's life with all the force of the winter storm howling outside her isolated cabin, they become trapped together in a cocoon of pleasure. Jason needs her to expose a con artist, and he also needs her kisses. Shell wants to trust him, but so much is at stake, including the secret that had finally brought her peace. Judy will leave you breathless with the elemental force raging between these two people.

On sale this month from FANFARE are three exciting novels. In **DAWN ON A JADE SEA** Jessica Bryan, the award-winning author of **ACROSS A WINE-DARK SEA,** once more intertwines romance, fantasy, and ancient history to create an utterly spellbinding story. Set against the stunning pageantry of ancient China, **DAWN ON A JADE SEA** brings together Rhea, a merperson from an undersea world, and Red Tiger, a son of merchants who has vowed revenge against the powerful nobleman who destroyed his family.

Now's your chance to grab a copy of **BLAZE,** by bestselling author Susan Johnson, and read the novel that won the *Romantic Times* award for Best Sensual Historical Romance and a Golden Certificate from *Affaire de Coeur* "for the quality, excellence of writing, entertainment and enjoyment it gave the readers." In this sizzling novel a Boston heiress is swept into a storm of passion she's never imagined, held spellbound by an Absarokee Indian who knows every woman's desires. . . .

Anytime we publish a book by Iris Johansen, it's an event—and **LAST BRIDGE HOME** shows why. Original, emotional, and sensual, it's romantic suspense at its most compelling. It begins with Jon Sandell, a man with many secrets and one remarkable power, appearing at Elizabeth Ramsey's cottage. When he reveals that he's there to protect her from danger, Elizabeth doesn't know whether this mesmerizing stranger is friend or foe. . . .

Also on sale this month in the Doubleday hardcover edition is **LADY DEFIANT** by Suzanne Robinson, a thrilling historical romance that brings back Blade, who was introduced in **LADY GALLANT.** Now Blade is one of Queen Elizabeth's most dangerous spies, and he must romance a beauty named Oriel who holds a clue that could alter the course of history.

Happy reading!

With warmest wishes,

Nita Taublib
Associate Publisher
LOVESWEPT and FANFARE

Don't miss these fabulous Bantam Fanfare
titles on sale in August.

DAWN ON A JADE SEA
by Jessica Bryan

BLAZE
by Susan Johnson

LAST BRIDGE HOME
by Iris Johansen

And in hardcover from Doubleday,
LADY DEFIANT
by Suzanne Robinson

DAWN ON A JADE SEA

by the award-winning author of
ACROSS A WINE-DARK SEA,

Jessica Bryan

She was a shimmering beauty from a kingdom of legend. A vision had brought Rhea to the glorious city of Ch'ang-an, compelling her to seek a green-eyed, auburn-haired foreign warrior called Zhao, the Red Tiger. Amid the jasmine of the Imperial Garden, passion will be born, hot as fire, strong as steel, eternal as the ocean tides . . .

A.D. 829.

The storm struck at midnight.

Nothing was spared. Not the tiny villages nestled along the coast, not the half-dozen fishing boats caught away from land, and not the caravan of the merchant who at sunset had ordered his men to camp beyond the hills that bordered the beach in an effort to avoid the worst of the storm.

As each man struggled through the frenzied night, one sound battered at his ears, making itself heard even over the mad tumult of wind and rain and thunder.

The sea.

Leading a sleepy-eyed horse through the early dawn, Zhao toiled along the last of the hills that overlooked the sea. Their progress had been slow, for the path along the low cliffs was narrow and rocky. The horse, its packs half-full with firewood scavenged in the aftermath of the storm, had to pick its way with care.

Suddenly the horse flung up his head, yet its gaze was not fixed on Zhao, but on the beach. The beast's ears swiveled nervously, his nostrils flared, then he shied and let out a resounding snort of alarm. Zhao froze. At the same moment that the horse had been frightened, something had called to him. Gripping the lead rope tightly in one hand, he used the other to soothe the animal as he stared across the sand.

The beach wound like a broad golden ribbon between the gray and green cliffs and the shimmering blue waters of the sea. Driftwood and debris from the storm lay scattered across it, as though thrown there by giant hands. Zhao saw nothing else, though the presence still called to him. He told himself it was only his imagination and was turning away when a soft sound, the merest whisper, came to him on the wind. The horse whinnied sharply, jerking his head so hard, the boy had to use both hands on the rope to prevent the beast from bolting.

Following the animal's gaze, he saw what he had missed before. Between a large boulder and a pile of driftwood lay a naked woman, her body almost hidden by the twin bulks of rock and wood. At the moment his gaze lit upon her, rays of the still-red sun struck the woman's entire body, bathing it in a scarlet mist, as deep and luminous as rubies.

Involuntarily he gasped aloud. Stumbling in his haste, he hurried down to the beach. By the time he reached her, the angle of the sun had changed, and the woman lay in shadow. Tethering the horse to a sturdy driftwood log, the boy knelt beside her. She was so still, Zhao thought her dead. Then he caught the faintest flicker of an eyelid, and he let out a deep sigh. In the whole of his fifteen years he had never seen an unclothed woman. The sight of her transfixed him, so that for several moments all he could do was stare. She was more magnificent than any living creature he had ever seen.

Strands of seaweed had threaded themselves through the glorious mantle of midnight-black hair that lay in wild profusion around her shoulders. More of the dark-green seaweed was draped across her throat and breasts. Though still shocked, Zhao noted that while the body belonged to a ripe woman, the face—with its clearly non-Han features—was that of a girl barely twenty. He also saw that the entire naked length of her had been darkened by the sun in a most unseemly manner, the smooth unblemished skin gleaming bronze-gold in the strong light.

Only the merest rise and fall of the woman's chest and an occasional fluttering of blue-veined eyelids indicated the presence of life. Although she was silent now, he knew the moan had come from her.

Slowly he reached out for one of the woman's arms. A strange shiver went through Zhao as he tentatively laid his fingers upon her limp arm. The woman's flesh was unexpectedly warm, and, astonished at himself, he felt his heartbeat quicken.

He would not have believed the woman could become any more beautiful. But at the touch of his hand, her long black eye lashes quivered and her eyes opened. Gray eyes. As silvery deep and beyond fathoming as a sea in winter.

Stunned, Zhao stared into the depths of those misty, enigmatic eyes. Though the woman was a stranger to him, he'd swear he saw a glimmer of recognition in her gaze. In the instant before she closed her eyes again, he knew his world had forever changed.

Trembling, he released the flaccid wrist he had been holding. Splashes of reddish-brown stained the sand beneath the woman's head. Looking closer, he saw that a deep gash, nearly hidden in the dark mass of her hair, was seeping blood. He drew in his breath. The woman needed help, but to move her without knowing the extent of her hurts could be even worse than not to help her at all.

He clambered to his feet. Ignoring the horse's plaintive whinny, he dashed off down the beach, running as though wings had attached themselves to his heels.

The caravan of Zhao's grand-uncle and head of the clan was not far from where the injured woman lay. But by the time he saw the hide tents and kneeling camels in the distance, Zhao was gulping for air, his lungs burning as if he were breathing fire. To his horror neither his grand-uncle nor his father—the only two men in the caravan with any knowledge of healing—were in camp.

He would have to take his father's healing pouch and care for the woman himself, he thought as he raced toward the tent he shared with his father. Until his elder relatives returned, there was no one he could trust with the discovery of a dazed and naked woman on the beach. Moments later he emerged from the tent and tore out of camp.

When he finally caught sight of his tethered horse, Zhao heaved a gasping prayer that the woman would still be alive.

Loaded down with the heavy pouch as well as a piece of satin to wrap her in, he stumbled toward the spot where she lay.

It was empty.

Only the bloodstained patch of sand showed that she had been there at all. He stared wildly around him, up at the cliffs, then toward the water. He saw her there, tall and proud-breasted, like some being not of this earth, wading deliberately into the sea.

"Lady!" he screamed as he ran toward her.

She glanced at him, a brief turning of that raven-maned head. In the bright sunlight he caught a glimpse of her eyes, silvery and strangely bright, like polished mirrors in the fierce glitter of sun and water. Then she dived.

"No, Lady, no!"

Frantically he threw himself forward. His arms grasped only air, and with a jarring thud he fell facedown in the wet sand. Leaping to his feet, he dashed into the sea, his gaze desperately searching the rolling waves. He saw her. She was swimming, but in a manner Zhao had never seen, nor even imagined possible.

Arms pressed close to her sides so that she resembled a pale-brown dolphin, the woman was undulating across the sapphire waves. Her body cut through the water with a speed and power that caused Zhao's next shout to strangle in his throat.

"La-lady," he croaked, then stood there in silence, watching her disappear. Unexpectedly a lump rose into his throat, and an inexplicable pain stabbed his breast. All around him he suddenly felt the presence of things unseen and not understood, but longed for nonetheless. Filled with grief and a strange yearning, he stood for a long time, ankle-deep in the shifting waves, gazing out to sea.

BLAZE
by
Susan Johnson

author of FORBIDDEN and SINFUL

The gold rush sparked a new American dream for those who staked their claims in the rich soil of undeveloped Indian territories. To Blaze Braddock, beautiful, pampered daughter of a millionaire, it was a chance to flee the stifling codes of Boston society. But when Jon Hazard Black, a proud young Absarokee chief, challenged her father's land claim, Blaze was swept up in a storm of passions she had never before even imagined . . .

When the evening star appeared in the sky, after a quiet if heated discussion, Hazard tied Blaze to him in two places, at waist and wrist, then lay down on the narrow bed and, exhausted, slept through the night for the first time in five days.

Lying very still, Blaze listened to Hazard's even breathing, until the slow, easy rhythm seemed part of her own respiration, until the warmth of the large man pressed close to her stole into her senses with an inexplicable rush of pleasure she could neither control nor deny. Cautiously she turned her head a millimeter in his direction, waited, then, observing no change in the deep, resonant breathing, slowly eased her glance around until he was fully within her gaze.

It came over her suddenly, as it always did—his unbearable beauty, the magnificence muted now in sleep to mere splendor. She watched him while the fading pastels of twilight disappeared into the void of night. Watched the play of light over the stark cheekbones, visually traced the perfect symmetry of finely chiseled nose. His sculptured mouth was prominently sensual—no austerity there, she noted. No, definitely not austere. And only with effort did she restrain herself from outlining that sensuous mouth with her fingertips. Even his brows were like delicate winged creatures, dark silky creatures that whispered to be touched. Blaze clenched her fingers tightly against the overpowering urge. And when his thick lashes fluttered suddenly, she caught her breath, fearful the sharp black eyes might open and find her own gaze transfixed. But he only sighed lightly, his fingers unconsciously tightening on the braided rawhide coiled around his hand.

As she observed him, taking in the sight and sound, the sage-sweet scent so much a part of these mountains it clung to everything, she suddenly saw, through unclouded vision, a different Hazard Black. Not the sensual, seductive man, as she had seen him, not the ruthless killer, as others saw him, not even an "Indian from an alien culture." She saw only a man, seeming as vulnerable as a child in his sleep. A man, beautiful beyond words but, transcending his physical perfection, beautiful in spirit, imbued with an indomitable courage, fearless against overwhelming odds. Odds any practical man would have refused. Jon Hazard Black had set himself against one of the most powerful mining cartels in the world. And he intended to stand his ground.

But later, in the roil and tumult of chaotic half sleep and black dreams, her logic and emotion at war, she felt the return of her initial outrage and resentment at his monumental arrogance at taking her hostage. How dare he, she thought with renewed vigor. *How the hell dare he!*

"You can't keep me here!" he heard her hiss as the first light of dawn appeared. Grunting softly, he rolled over, still half asleep, and the braided leather rope binding them tightened. The movement brought her hard against his back. He vaguely heard a quiet gasp and felt her stiffen. Then silence. Blessed silence, he thought, recalling her volatile temper.

She repeated the phrase in a scathing whisper. He opened one eye briefly, casting a glance over his bare shoulder, and encountered snapping blue eyes. "Sorry," he murmured truthfully, for he knew already that his life had become endlessly complicated because of one Miss Venetia Braddock.

"Sorry? *You're* sorry?" she muttered incredulously. And then proceeded to read him the riot act until he exasperatedly answered in his own rush of temper, *"Enough!"*

But she wouldn't stop, the words tumbling out, furious and hot with defiance, like clubs beating and flailing at his head. He had to kiss her to arrest the torrent of abusive rage. A hand over her mouth might have worked as well, he admitted as his lips covered hers, but logic relinquished the field hastily to an unexplained desire to quiet her in a more pleasurable way.

She tasted sweet and welcoming, he thought, settling himself in an unconsciously fluid maneuver between her legs. How warm she was . . . and soft. Loosening the coiled rope from his hand, his fingers tangled in the silk of her hair, holding her like a precious gift, while his lips and tongue explored the luscious interior of her mouth.

He couldn't help himself. Didn't want to. She was here, his for the taking. And in a flashing second he realized how much he'd missed having a woman near. She felt like homecoming and rapture and soul-deep solace. When he raised his mouth the idyll was shattered.

"You . . . you . . . animal," she sputtered, her head turning fitfully in his grasp, her eyes glowering. "You odious, abominable—"

". . . savage," he finished softly and took her mouth again. This time in a hard, possessive invasion that put to use all the expertise acquired so pleasurably over the years. When he lifted his mouth a second time, long minutes later, his slow, sure skill had left her trembling and breathless. The sputter, modified, was now more like a sigh.

"This . . . will . . . never . . ."

". . . get any gold mined," Hazard whispered, a smile curling through the words. "You're right, *sweet bia* . . . and I'll try to get you into the kitchen very soon"—his smile widened—"so you can make me breakfast. Are you ready to begin earning your keep?" He tugged her closer with the rawhide still tied around her waist.

She didn't answer at first. Couldn't. Didn't want to. Didn't know her own mind. But his fingers slipped between her thighs and slid upward like devil's sorcery, very slowly at first, tantalizing, waiting for her to ask for more. And when she arched her hips in response, his slim fingers eased into her sweetness. She cried out and reached for him, her arms twining tightly around his neck.

He raised himself slightly against the pressure of her hands and, looking down at her exquisite, flushed face, asked again, "Are you ready to earn your keep?" His fingers continued to stroke languidly and she moaned softly with each delicate movement. Bending near, his lips hovered in a whisper above hers. "Say yes, little rich girl." His fingers drifted deeper and her nails dug into his shoulders. "Say you'll cook for me."

His obliging movements stopped and she quickly whispered, "Yes."

"And clean for me."

"Yes," she breathed.

"And do anything else."

"Oh—please, yes."

His fingers slid free and he moved over her gently.

"Now," she cried.

"Soon," he said and eased his body down.

The next half-formed plea died in a breathy moan as he glided, hard and long, into her urging womanly warmth. How could she, he thought with pleasure, feel so excruciatingly fine?

How could he, she thought, with a shameful thrill, arching against his spearing invasion, know I want him so?

An hour later, when the rawhide shackle had long since been untied by gentle fingers, and when Jon Hazard Black had given in to his hostage's demands as many times as any able man would, he kissed her one last time, rose from the shambles of the bed, and said, "I'm going to bathe in the stream behind the cabin. Would you care to join me?"

"Is it cold?"

"Brisk."

"I know mountain streams. No, thank you."

He smiled. "Suit yourself. Breakfast in ten minutes?"

"Is that an invitation?"

"Not exactly. Call it . . . a diplomatic request." He could see the stubborn set of her jaw begin to form. "Very diplomatic," he cajoled, reaching down to touch her pretty mouth with a placating finger. "Relax, Boston, I'm no ogre. I'll help."

"Then let me go," Blaze said in a hurried rushing breath, fearful of staying with him for reasons that had nothing at all to do with mining claims.

Hazard's half-lowered eyelids covered eyes so dark they were unreadable. "I wish I could," he said quietly, "but the battle lines have been drawn. I'm afraid it's too late."

"You're serious."

Hazard paused a moment before answering. "You've led a

sheltered life, Boston," he finally said. Tossing a towel around his neck, he continued in a moderate tone, as though discussing the merits of calling cards as a social gesture. "They're out to kill me. I consider that serious. That's why you're here. And that's why you're staying." A sudden flash of white teeth seemed to discount the undercurrent of danger. "I like my eggs soft-boiled."

He was gone in a noiseless tread, and she lay there stunned for several minutes. People didn't actually kill each other over a small section of mountain land, did they? Certainly not her father and his friends. Did they? For the first time a quiver of doubt intruded.

Wrapping the sheet around her, Blaze walked to the window and, looking out, glimpsed Hazard half screened by a clump of pines. He was swimming in a small pool contrived by damming up a portion of the rushing mountain stream. The sunlight shone off his sleek wet hair. Then he submerged, only to reappear moments later long yards away, shaking his head, droplets of water spraying like crystals from his streaming black hair.

When he started back to the cabin, all slender grace and hard rising muscle, Blaze went to the door, intending to meet him as a friendly gesture. After all, if she was truly a hostage—and it appeared the case; there was never equivocation when Hazard spoke, no matter how quiet the tone—she might as well be gracious about it. She pulled on the door latch. The door didn't respond. She tugged more determinedly. Nothing. She swore. Damn his untrusting soul. He'd locked her in!

LAST BRIDGE HOME
by
Iris Johansen

bestselling author of
THE GOLDEN BARBARIAN
and THE WIND DANCER trilogy

*Jon Sandell is a man with many secrets and one remarkable
power, the ability to read a woman's mind, to touch her soul, to
know her every waking desire. His vital mission is to rescue a
woman unaware of the danger she is in. But who will protect
her from him?*

She inhaled sharply as she spotted a man standing on the
stone steps at the front door of the cottage. A man she had
never seen before.

She pulled her car into the driveway and slowed it to a stop.
The man, who was coming down the steps now, didn't look
menacing, but he didn't look like the Caspar Milquetoast type
either. There was something very controlled about his deliberate approach. Controlled. What an odd word to come to mind,
she thought. His deeply tanned face was completely impassive,
yet she had the impression he was exerting a tremendous effort
to subdue forces that were seething below the surface of his
calm exterior.

Standing beside her window, he bent down slightly to look at
her. He spoke in a tone a level above normal so she could hear
through the glass. "I'm glad you're being cautious. It's very
lonely out here for a woman alone. I've been waiting for you."

He was gazing at her with an odd, almost hungry, intentness.
The thought that he was only inches away, separated from her
by a flimsy sheet of glass, sent a sudden shudder of fear through
her. His eyes were darkly brilliant, his black brows heavy, and
his bone structure was too strongly defined to ever be termed

handsome. Strength. A strength so powerful it was a shock to her senses. She found herself staring at him in wide-eyed fascination.

He frowned. "For God's sake, stop looking at me like that." His voice was rough and slightly husky. "I'm not going to hurt you. I'm here to help you. I'd never—" He broke off and drew a deep breath. "Look, I'm sorry if I startled you. Let's begin again. My name is Jon Sandell and Mark Ramsey was my cousin. Perhaps he mentioned me?"

Jon Sandell. She felt a swift swell of relief and hurriedly rolled down the window. "Of course he did. I'm very glad to meet you at last." She grinned and wrinkled her nose at him. "Though you probably think I'm flighty as a loon to treat you as if you were Charles Manson. I'm not usually this uptight. I guess I have a case of prenatal jitters." She opened the door and swung her khaki-clad legs carefully to the ground. It was a massive undertaking for her to get herself out from behind the steering wheel these days. Jon Sandell stepped forward and lifted her easily from the seat and onto her feet.

"Oh, thank you, that helped a lot. I'll be with you in just a minute. I have to get the groceries out of the car. I stopped at the supermarket on the way home from school, which delayed me a bit. Have you been waiting long?"

"No." He was frowning again. "You shouldn't be out here by yourself. It may have been all right before, but now that you're—"

"—big as a house," she finished for him. She shut the car door and went around to the back of the station wagon. "This is my home. Where else would I go?" She unlocked and opened the gate. "Besides, I'm not alone. The Spauldings have a farm two miles down the road, and I have Sam."

"Sam?"

"Sam is my Heinz 57," she said with a gentle smile. "He's half Great Dane and half I-don't-know-what. Will you stay for dinner? I put a stew in the Crockpot this morning. There will be plenty for two."

He shook his head. "I can't stay but I'd like a cup of coffee and a little conversation, if it's not too much trouble."

She shook her head as she turned and headed for the steps. "Of course it's not too much trouble. I'd like to talk to you too." She glanced back over her shoulder as she unlocked the heavy

Dutch door. A smile lit her face with glowing warmth, and she said, "Mark was a stranger in these parts and not many people got to know him well enough to realize how wonderful he was. I think one of the things I missed most after he died was not being able to talk to someone who loved him as much as I did."

He was gazing at her face with the same intent expression she had noticed earlier. "I wanted to come to you then, but they wouldn't let me."

"I understood why you couldn't come to the funeral. Mark had told me you are out of the country most of the time."

"That's a fairly accurate way of phrasing it. Well, I'm here now. Why don't you go inside."

His last words were a command, spoken with the casual confidence of someone accustomed to being obeyed. Whoever "they" were, they must have been exceptionally high up in the echelon of Sandell's company to prevent him from doing anything he wanted to do. She saluted. "I'll put the coffee on, sir."

He looked up, and for the flicker of a moment there was a warm smile on his hard face. "Was I being authoritarian? I was in the military for a while and I guess you never really lose a sense of command."

"I guess you don't." She swung open the door and left it ajar for him as she moved briskly down the hall to the large kitchen which stretched the length of the rear of the cottage.

"Do you use milk or sugar?"

"No."

"Neither do I. I like my coffee black as sin and loaded with caffeine. I've been drinking it without caffeine lately because it's better for the baby, but I still miss the pick-me-up it gave me." One hand absently rubbed the hollow of her spine as she made the coffee. "And weighing as much as I do these days, it takes a heck of a lot to pick me u—" She broke off as she turned to face him. "You're looking at me very oddly. Is something wrong?"

"No. I was just thinking how beautiful you are."

She laughed with genuine amusement. "I'm not even pretty. Lord, you must have been out of the country and away from civilization and women for a long time. Where were you anyway? In the wilds of the Sahara? Remind me to introduce you to my neighbor, Serena Spaulding. She's simply gorgeous."

She took the coffee carafe and crossed the room to where he was standing. "But thanks anyway for trying to make a fat, pregnant lady feel good." She poured the steaming liquid into two cups and turned to set the carafe on the warmer. "Take off your coat and sit down." She shrugged out of her heavy navy peacoat. "I'll be right back. I have to call Sam and tell him it's chow time."

"I wouldn't think a Great Dane would have to be told."

"Usually he doesn't." Her brow knitted with a frown. "I don't know why he wasn't here to meet me. I'll be right back."

She returned in less than five minutes. "He didn't come when I called." She came slowly toward him, the worried frown still on her face. "Crazy dog. He's probably out chasing rabbits again."

Sitting down across from him at the round oak table, she straightened her shoulders as if to shrug off a burden. "Sorry, I seem to be on an anxiety kick lately. I've been blaming it on Andrew. He can't talk back yet."

"Andrew?"

"My son. It's a boy. I asked the doctor for an amniocentesis; it's a test that detects any genetic or other problems and spins off the fascinating information of the sex of the unborn child." She looked down at her coffee, her index finger gently rubbing the side of the cup. "After Mark died I needed more than a faceless entity to share my body. I needed to know my baby was all right, as well as a real person, a companion." She lifted her eyes to meet his gaze. "Do you understand?"

"Yes."

He said nothing else, yet she felt a warmth sweep through her unlike anything she had ever known. For a moment it seemed impossible to tear her gaze away from his. Her throat felt tight and she had difficulty breathing. She picked up her cup and cradled it in her palms. "I think you do. I guess it's not surprising. Mark was the most understanding man I've ever met. It must run in the family."

"I'm nothing like Mark." His tone was suddenly harsh. "Don't make the mistake of drawing comparisons that aren't there. We were as different as night and day." His lips twisted. "Inside as well as out."

What he said was true. Physically there was no resemblance between him and Mark. Jon Sandell was only a few inches taller than her five feet eight and Mark had been well over six feet. Mark also had had golden coloring with deep blue eyes and a smile as kind as summer rain. He was so incredibly handsome that people had stopped on the street to stare at him in bedazzlement. She had been dazzled herself at first and hadn't been able to believe it when he started to pursue her with gentle persistence.

There was nothing either gentle or golden about his cousin. Jon Sandell was dark and intense and composed of hard, sharp angles. She found her gaze drawn to the strong brown column of his throat and allowed it to wander down to catch the faintest glimpse of virile dark hair above the top button of his navy flannel shirt. The dark thatch of hair looked soft, springy, and suddenly, incredibly, she found her palms tingling as if she were actually touching it. The shocking sensation caused her to quickly jerk her gaze away. What had happened to her? For a moment she had felt a burst of sensuality stronger than any she had previously experienced. It was nothing, she told herself. Jon Sandell projected a raw sexuality that would have aroused a response in any woman. I didn't mean anything. Still, for a moment, along with the sensuality, she had felt a closeness, almost a bonding that was, in many ways, like the empathy she had known with Mark. "Well, I'm sure you're as kind as Mark or you wouldn't be making this courtesy call. I'm really grateful, Mr. Sandell."

"Jon. I've thought of you as Elizabeth for a long time." He sipped his coffee. "And I'm not kind. I'm here because I want to be." He paused. "And because I have to be."

LADY DEFIANT
by Suzanne Robinson
author of
LADY GALLANT and LADY HELLFIRE

Set during the tumultuous Elizabethan era in England, LADY DEFIANT tells the story of Blade, first introduced in LADY GALLANT. The disarmingly handsome Blade, now one of Queen Elizabeth's most dangerous spies, is given the task of romancing a clever young beauty named Oriel. She unknowingly holds a clue that could alter the course of history, bringing Mary, Queen of Scots to the throne of England. LADY DEFIANT is a thrilling, sensual romance from the increasingly popular Suzanne Robinson.

On sale in hardcover from Doubleday in August.
On sale in paperback from Bantam FANFARE in December.

OFFICIAL RULES TO WINNERS CLASSIC SWEEPSTAKES

No Purchase necessary. To enter the sweepstakes follow instructions found elsewhere in this offer. You can also enter the sweepstakes by hand printing your name, address, city, state and zip code on a 3" x 5" piece of paper and mailing it to: Winners Classic Sweepstakes, P.O. Box 785, Gibbstown, NJ 08027. Mail each entry separately. Sweepstakes begins 12/1/91. Entries must be received by 6/1/93. Some presentations of this sweepstakes may feature a deadline for the Early Bird prize. If the offer you receive does, then to be eligible for the Early Bird prize your entry must be received according to the Early Bird date specified. Not responsible for lost, late, damaged, misdirected, illegible or postage due mail. Mechanically reproduced entries are not eligible. All entries become property of the sponsor and will not be returned.

Prize Selection/Validations: Winners will be selected in random drawings on or about 7/30/93, by VENTURA ASSOCIATES, INC., an independent judging organization whose decisions are final. Odds of winning are determined by total number of entries received. Circulation of this sweepstakes is estimated not to exceed 200 million. Entrants need not be present to win. All prizes are guaranteed to be awarded and delivered to winners. Winners will be notified by mail and may be required to complete the affidavit of eligibility and release of liability which must be returned within 14 days of date of notification or alternate winners will be selected. Any guest of a trip winner will also be required to execute a release of liability. Any prize notification letter or any prize returned to a participating sponsor, Bantam Doubleday Dell Publishing Group, Inc., its participating divisions or subsidiaries, or VENTURA ASSOCIATES, INC. as undeliverable will be awarded to an alternate winner. Prizes are not transferable. No multiple prize winners except as may be necessary due to unavailability, in which case a prize of equal or greater value will be awarded. Prizes will be awarded approximately 90 days after the drawing. All taxes, automobile license and registration fees, if applicable, are the sole responsibility of the winners. Entry constitutes permission (except where prohibited) to use winners' names and likenesses for publicity purposes without further or other compensation.

Participation: This sweepstakes is open to residents of the United States and Canada, except for the province of Quebec. This sweepstakes is sponsored by Bantam Doubleday Dell Publishing Group, Inc. (BDD), 666 Fifth Avenue, New York, NY 10103. Versions of this sweepstakes with different graphics will be offered in conjunction with various solicitations or promotions by different subsidiaries and divisions of BDD. Employees and their families of BDD, its division, subsidiaries, advertising agencies, and VENTURA ASSOCIATES, INC., are not eligible.

Canadian residents, in order to win, must first correctly answer a time limited arithmetical skill testing question. Void in Quebec and wherever prohibited or restricted by law. Subject to all federal, state, local and provincial laws and regulations.

Prizes: The following values for prizes are determined by the manufacturers' suggested retail prices or by what these items are currently known to be selling for at the time this offer was published. Approximate retail values include handling and delivery of prizes. Estimated maximum retail value of prizes: 1 Grand Prize ($27,500 if merchandise or $25,000 Cash); 1 First Prize ($3,000); 5 Second Prizes ($400 each); 35 Third Prizes ($100 each); 1,000 Fourth Prizes ($9.00 each) ; 1 Early Bird Prize ($5,000); Total approximate maximum retail value is $50,000. Winners will have the option of selecting any prize offered at level won. Automobile winner must have a valid driver's license at the time the car is awarded. Trips are subject to space and departure availability. Certain black-out dates may apply. Travel must be completed within one year from the time the prize is awarded. Minors must be accompanied by an adult. Prizes won by minors will be awarded in the name of parent or legal guardian.

For a list of Major Prize Winners (available after 7/30/93): send a self-addressed, stamped envelope entirely separate from your entry to: Winners Classic Sweepstakes Winners, P.O. Box 825, Gibbstown, NJ 08027. Requests must be received by 6/1/93. DO NOT SEND ANY OTHER CORRESPONDENCE TO THIS P.O. BOX.

The Delaney Dynasty lives on in

The Delaney Christmas Carol

by Kay Hooper, Iris Johansen, & Fayrene Preston

Three of romantic fiction's best-loved authors present the changing face of Christmas spirit—past, present, and future—as they tell the story of three generations of Delaneys in love.

CHRISTMAS PAST by Iris Johansen

From the moment he first laid eyes on her, Kevin Delaney felt a curious attraction for the ragclad Gypsy beauty rummaging through the attic of his ranch at Killara. He didn't believe for a moment her talk of magic mirrors and second-sight, but something about Zara St. Cloud stirred his blood. Now, as Christmas draws near, a touch leads to a kiss and a gift of burning passion.

CHRISTMAS PRESENT by Fayrene Preston

Bria Delaney had been looking for Christmas ornaments in her mother's attic, when she saw him in the mirror for the first time—a stunningly handsome man with sky-blue eyes and red-gold hair. She had almost convinced herself he was only a dream when Kells Braxton arrived at Killara and led them both to a holiday wonderland of sensuous pleasure.

CHRISTMAS FUTURE by Kay Hooper

As the last of the Delaney men, Brett returned to Killara this Christmastime only to find it in the capable hands of his father's young and beautiful widow. Yet the closer he got to Cassie, the more Brett realized that the embers of their old love still burned and that all it would take was a look, a kiss, a caress, to turn their dormant passion into an inferno.

 The best in Women's Fiction from Bantam FANFARE.
On sale in November 1992 AN 428 8/92